« Love, Sara »

<< Love,
Sara >>

MARY

BETH

LUNDGREN

Henry Holt and Company :) New York

Unending thanks to the following whose book it is as much as mine:

My husband and first reader, Ted, whose love is everything.

Lila, Susan, and Kathy—generous, irreplaceable critique group, and friends. Their abilities and willingness to tear Sara's story apart allowed me to see how to put it together.

Maeve, who gave me Sara's voice and so much more.

Colin, Erin, Gabe, and Melissa, whose honest criticisms provided teen perspective.

Trudy, Eileen, Moira, Margaret, Mary Ann, Lisa, Anna, and Dottie, who read and commented on the book at various stages.

Barbara Kouts, my agent, who loved Sara as soon as she met her.

Nina Ignatowicz, my editor, who insisted the book could be better. As always, she was right.

David Rohlfing, assistant editor—capable, patient, and calm—who guided both Sara and me through the intricate process from manuscript to printed book.

Dave Caplan, whose book design brought Sara's writing to life.

Rosa, who taught me that whatever the beginning, survival is possible.

Maggie, who began it all.

Thanks also to: Martha Collins, author of "The Story We Know," who gave permission to use her poem, and who helped Sara title one of hers.

Dan Castellanos, M.D., Director of Psychiatry for Children and Adolescents, and Chief of Pediatric Mental Health Emergency at the Mental Health Hospital at the University of Miami (Florida), Jackson Memorial Medical Center. He shared with me his intimate knowledge of teen suicide attempts and their aftermath.

Henry Holt and Company, LLC, *Publishers since 1866*
115 West 18th Street, New York, New York 10011
Henry Holt is a registered trademark of Henry Holt and Company, LLC
Copyright © 2001 by Mary Beth Lundgren. All rights reserved.
Distributed in Canada by H. B. Fenn and Company Ltd.

Library of Congress Cataloging-in-Publication Data
Lundgren, Mary Beth. Love, Sara / Mary Beth Lundgren.   p.   cm.
Summary: In a series of e-mails and journal entries Sara, a high school junior with a history of sexual abuse and foster home care, reveals her feelings about herself and two friends who are headed for destruction.
[1. Friendship—Fiction. 2. Foster home care—Fiction. 3. Suicide—Fiction. 4. High schools—Fiction. 5. Schools—Fiction. 6. E-mail—Fiction. 7. Letters—Fiction. 8. Diaries—Fiction.]
I. Title.   PZ7.L978848 Lo 2001   [Fic]—dc21   2001024015

ISBN 0-8050-6797-3 / First Edition—2001
Printed in the United States of America on acid-free paper. ∞
10 9 8 7 6 5 4 3 2 1

Permission for the use of the following is gratefully acknowledged:
Cleveland State University Poetry Center (for Martha Collins) for "The Story We Know" from *The Catastrophe of Rainbows*, by Martha Collins, copyright © 1985 by Martha Collins.

Dedicated to the million children who suffer abuse each year, the thousands of children with special needs who wait for homes, and to the survivors.

* * * * *

A plea, from my heart, to any teen in the midst of a crisis:

Tell an adult who cares about you. Wait! It WILL be better tomorrow.

«Love, Sara»

* *

From the computer files of Sara J. Reichert:
my life, from the last day of summer vacation
to almost-spring of my junior year.

No matter what you might have heard,
this is the real story.

* *

From: Sara Reichert [enigma22@ezmail.com]
Date: Tues, 1 Sept 1998 21:16:54 EST
To: Dulciana Newton [DANcer@ezmail.com]
Subject: PRISON SENTENCE

Hey Dulcie! Can you believe how fast everything changes? We're lyin in the sun a few
hours ago, chillin, listening to our music.
And now I'm tryin to get my head ready fer
you know what.

HATE the first day of school. HATE IT! OK, I
know it's childish. So shoot me.

Talk yer way out of chem class yet with the
parent-people?

Speaking of . . . Carol HAS to be having PMS.
I'll be here 4 years in Jan—you'd think I'd
be used to her family meetins by now.
Wrong! She always wants to know my inner-
most thoughts and feelings. "How do I feel
about school tomorrow?" she asks. I say,
"Fine." She pops like a balloon. "You can't
ALWAYS be fine," she says. Like I'd tell her

5

my stomach's totally heaving at the thought of Honors English, esp the creative writing part.

You I can tell—what if I can't do it?

Hey! In that witchin yellow shirt you are one stylin chic. Gonna wear it tomorrow?

Love, Sara

P.S. Sorry about the venting.

<<*He's simply got the instinct for being unhappy highly developed.*>>
—Saki (H. H. Munro)

From: Dulciana Newton [DANcer@ezmail.com]
Date: Tues, 1 Sept 1998 22:10:15 EST
To: Sara Reichert [enigma22@ezmail.com]
Subject: RE: PRISON SENTENCE

Sara, where do you find those quotes? That one is choice! But, hey, ya gotta look at the up side. :)

School's okay by me. At least we're JRs this year.

My 'rents say I'll never get into a good college without chem, so I HAVE to take it. This Asian-oppression thing is laughable. They say I have to "honor my Korean heritage." Can you spell *stereotype*? They adopted me when I was 2 yrs old!!! I'm American, not Korean. And what do they know about Korea anyway? You: No chem—one good thing about having a foster 'rent stead of a real one, right? :) I refuse to let mine get to me.

Another upper—YOU passed your driver's test. I am GREEN, girl!

You'll do fine in H Eng. And I'll help, IF you need me.

Savin my yellow shirt for pep rally Thursday—JON will be there—omigod!—he just rocks my world. I heard that band Hot Mustard is gonna play so I talked to 'em and—TA-DA! I MIGHT sing with 'em. GR8, yes?

Life is good!

Pick ya up in the A.M. 8:00?

Dulcie

From: Sara Reichert [enigma22@ezmail.com]
Date: Tues, 1 Sept 1998 22:20:54 EST
To: Dulciana Newton [DANcer@ezmail.com]
Subject: RE: RE: PRISON SENTENCE

Dulcie—Can you spell *Pollyanna*?

Life is life!

I hear you about diggin Jon 'n stuff, but he's such a JOCK!!!!

And I hear ya about H Eng. We'll see. . . .

As for the A.M. Better make it ¼ to 8. Don't ferget waitin fer that friggin train to cross Columbia Ave.

From: Sara Reichert [enigma22@ezmail.com]
Date: Tues, 1 Sept 1998 23:20:43 EST
To: Dulciana Newton [DANcer@ezmail.com]
Subject: AWFUL NEWS

Dulcie—This is terrible. TV news just said Tim Willis—he's one of the football players we talked to at the quarry—was killed in a car crash tonight.

S

From: Dulciana Newton [DANcer@ezmail.com]
Date: Tues, 1 Sept 1998 23:30:15 EST
To: Sara Reichert [enigma22@ezmail.com]
Subject: RE: AWFUL NEWS

Thank God it wasn't Jon. He must be crushed. Why is life so sad sometimes?

Dulcie

From: Sara Reichert [enigma22@ezmail.com]
Date: Tues, 1 Sept 1998 23:40:43 EST
To: Dulciana Newton [DANcer@ezmail.com]
Subject: RE: RE: AWFUL NEWS

D—Have you seen this poem by Martha Collins? Maybe it'll help.

<<THE STORY WE KNOW>>

The way to begin is always the same. Hello, / Hello. Your hand, your name. So glad, Just fine, / and Good-bye at the end. That's every story we know,

and why pretend? But lunch tomorrow? / No?

9

Yes? An omelette, salad, chilled white wine?
/ The way to begin is simple, sane, Hello,

and then it's Sunday, coffee, the *Times*, a
slow / day by the fire, dinner at eight or
nine / and Good-bye. In the end, this is
the story we know

so well we don't turn the page, or look
below / the picture, or follow the words to
the next line: / The way to begin is always
the same. Hello.

But one night, through the latticed window,
snow / begins to whiten the air, and the
tall white pine. / Good-bye is the end of
every story we know

that night, and when we close the curtains,
oh, / we hold each other against that cold
white sign / of the way we all begin and
end. *Hello*, / *Good-bye* is the only story.
We know, we know.

From: Dulciana Newton [DANcer@ezmail.com]
Date: Tues, 1 Sept 1998 23:55:15 EST
To: Sara Reichert [enigma22@ezmail.com]
Subject: RE:RE:RE: AWFUL NEWS

Sara,

Thanks. Beautiful. But I don't quite get
it. Explain it to me sometime?

D

My Journal, My Life

TUESDAY NIGHT, SEPTEMBER 1, 1998

MONSIEUR HENRI DE TOULOUSE-LAUTREC
CAFÉ DES ARTISTES
LEFT BANK
PARIS, FRANCE

Mon Cher Monsieur Henri,
Writing to "Dear Diary" seems childish, so I hope it's OK if I write to you instead. You're my hero ever since I read a biography of you and saw that old movie of your life. I've got a few questions:

1. *How could you, a famous artist, bear to scoot around Paris kneeling on a wooden cart not much bigger than a skateboard? I would have been so embarrassed.*
2. *Your posters are fabulous. How did you decide that art should be your life?*

12

*3. And after you became famous, why did you keep on
   drinking?*

*Hey, I know that you're dead, but maybe you'll hear me?
Maybe by explaining my life to you as it happens, I'll figure it
out. So here goes.*

This is me in a nutshell:

*Hard to believe—stay with me now—
Sara, the human yo-yo
is at the same school and has the same friend
for the second year in a row.*

*Wow! You can't possibly understand how truly amazing
that is.*

A helpful, I hope, definition:

*enigma (en ig´ ma), n.: a person of puzzling or contra-
dictory character*

That's me—an enigma.

*I doubt anybody really understands me, even Dulcie (she's
my first-ever friend). How could they unless they'd lived my
life? God knows, I don't even understand me sometimes.*

*Here's my question for tonight: Will Dulcie still be my
friend this time next week?*

*We stopped on the way home from swimming at the
quarry for a cappuccino at our favorite coffee shop. Some*

senior named Jon Draper—he's the team quarterback—stopped at our table with his buds Ted and Anthony. Dulcie went totally ga-ga over Jon.

She and I are SO close. I didn't think I'd ever have a friend, and then I found Dulcie in English class last year.

At first, we were real competitive—she's a super writer, and I'm just learning. I felt sorry for her too. Other kids laughed at her, even though she's really pretty. She has this kind of limp, I guess because she had a clubfoot when she was born. She's also a year younger, because she skipped ninth grade.

Then, when we were working together on an advertising project, I don't know why, but Blair Dillard—she's at a private school this year—called Dulcie a "gook," and Dulcie's face looked like somebody'd kicked her in the stomach. I lost it. My hip "accidentally" knocked over Blair's desk.

Blair yells, "Hey!"

Of course I say, "Oops. So sorry."

Her eyes make slits she's so mad. But nobody messes with me, not even Blair. (They call me "the Beast" sometimes, but I couldn't care less.) Blair's buds help her pick up all her stuff, and that's that.

Since then, nobody has messed with Dulcie either. Her smile was all the thank-you I needed. But she sent a note, too, on a beautiful card with 67 Cleveland, Ohio (that's where I live), buildings painted on it. I framed it and hung it on my wall.

Now I'm afraid that if she starts seeing this guy, she won't have time for me. That's selfish, but I want you to know the bad parts of me, too.

Here's how it is with my current "family": Carol Reilly, my foster mom, is a good person, basically, and smart. I mean, her husband died, but still, we live in this nice house in a suburb.

She's tough—went in the army after graduating from high school—and pretty much gets what she wants. Why did she want me? Good question. I don't know how it was in your time, but now they're desperate for foster parents. Everybody wants those cute babies, but nobody wants us older kids.

Carol already had two kids, a mother, three sisters, and friends. No boyfriends though—too busy, she says.

She stopped playing drill sergeant this summer. Don't have to report to her every five minutes like before. Don't have to take care of her kids—Hannah and Keith—every day.

She even bought me my own PC, and networked it to hers, with a server and everything. She's a computer consultant and needs this stuff for her business, so it's not as if she did it for me, but still. . . .

She's 180 degrees from me. I'm quiet, and Carol's a talker. She's small and pretty—blond curly hair and blue eyes—I'm big and not. Of course I shower every day, and my hair's long and shiny, but it's plain brown and straighter than string. I hate makeup, and I could lose 20 pounds.

And, while I pretty much go along with whatever, Carol wants to manage the world. Of course I don't say that to her. Believe me, making waves with a foster parent gets you in trouble.

Carol's current thing is about my style.

Please! Everybody wears combat boots. I don't say that to her either. But I will not wear those THINGS she brings home from garage sales—little flat shoes, a pink nightshirt with cutesy cats, a navy blue–striped sweater that's too tight. Baggy's my thing, and she wants me to wear GIRL STUFF!

About her kids—Keith is OK if you like six-year-olds. He slams every door, jumps off every step, and drives you crazy with his questions!

And then there's Hannah—two minutes around her and I want to scream. She's a pouter, and her biggest problem in life is being bored, so she follows me around all the time. Well, OK, her father died five years ago, and that's terrible. But my experience with fathers? She might be better off. I know that sounds cold, but you don't know all about me yet.

Anyway, did I cry all the time when I was twelve? No! I was afraid to do anything at that age, much less cry. I was scared to death Carol would send me back to Elmwood (in your time, they would have called it an orphanage) like the Thomases did. And the Andersons. And the Bakers. Wonder if evil Ronnie Baker ever told his mother the truth about who killed their dog? I think people who abuse animals should have the same things they did done to them.

Time for bed. Carol just yelled upstairs, says she's told me for the last time. Hope so. More soon.

Good night, Henri.

Sara

P.S.

> *Jon the Jock, a sparrow hawk,*
> *But cute, I guess,*
> *More or less.*
> *Too bad.*
> *Squawk!*

My Journal, My Life

MONSIEUR HENRI DE TOULOUSE-LAUTREC
CAFÉ DES ARTISTES
LEFT BANK
PARIS, FRANCE

Mon Cher Monsieur Henri,

Hey, I'm glad I'm writing instead of talking to you because I've got a cold, and my nose and throat are sore.

So, where were we? Oh, yeah, I was telling you about all the families I've lived with.

After the Bakers, who, except for Ronnie, probably still think I killed their dog, I lived with the Landers. I really thought Marianne and Tom were going to work out. I guess they believed it, too; said they were adopting me, so right away I made sure to call them Mom and Dad. Big mistake!

Every day I took a bus to that old green-paint-on-every-wall, run-down school. And every day my teacher called

Marianne. They put me in a Special Ed class—said I was hyperactive, unable to concentrate. All she talked about was how I disturbed her precious class, couldn't sit still, etc.

Please! I was twelve years old and totally screwed up. What did the teacher expect?!

Marianne helped me with homework, and Tom read to me from The Hobbit—his favorite book by J. R. R. Tolkien. Said it would help me focus. It was an exciting book. That's what got me started reading. At first, I sat on his lap (one of my many therapists said I was being seductive—normal given my background—but today I can't believe I did that). Of course, Tom tensed up every time. And I learned. After a couple times, I sat next to him instead.

A month later, Marianne and Tom said the same old words: Not your fault. Not anyone's fault. Just didn't work out.

They took me back to Elmwood the day after Thanksgiving. That's almost five years ago now.

After that, I stopped crying.

Anyway, this is my last try at a family. If this doesn't work, I'll have to live at Elmwood till I'm eighteen. Then I'll be on my own.

I think Carol trusts me now, at least not to burn myself with cigarettes, or to try to kill myself. I was just so angry and confused that day when Marianne and Tom got rid of me.

I told them I'd forgotten something in my room, and grabbed a bottle of pills from their medicine chest. After "lights out" at Elmwood that night, I swallowed them. I guess one of the staff found me and rushed me to the hospital.

I don't remember much, but I do remember this: You throw up forever after they pump your stomach, and your nose and throat are raw meat from that damn tube they shove up your nose and down your throat (twice! in my case).

Who knew an orange Popsicle could taste so good?

Here's what I know, Henri: Alone is like, all of a sudden, you're dropped into Afghanistan. Everyone is different from you. Everything is terrifying, dangerous. Everything you do is wrong. No one understands you. Nobody wants you, nobody cares. There's nowhere to go.

I promise you, Henri: I will NOT EVER be alone again. I CANNOT go back to not having a friend.

Anyway, Carol came along a few months later. If I ever get like that again, she'll probably want me to see a therapist for the rest of my life. If that means I live, so be it.

We have a lot in common, Henri. Just like me, you had parents who shouldn't have had children. You knew people that society didn't approve of. You were an outsider, too.

It's wonderful that you loved those forgotten girls of Paris nightlife, and made them immortal. Maybe I'll make someone famous one day with my writing. Maybe you'll get totally tired of hearing about me, me, me. Hope not.

Your friend (you feel like one to me already),

Sara

P.S.

*The life of every man is a diary in which he means to
write one story, and writes another. . . .*

—Sir J. M. Barrie

P.P.S. Can you tell I like quotes? I bought a quotations dictionary with my birthday money from Carol last year. Birthday money! Can you believe it? Like, doesn't everybody get birthday money? Sure!

From: Dulciana Newton [DANcer@ezmail.com]
Date: Thurs, 3 Sept 1998 18:35:15 EST
To: Sara Reichert [enigma22@ezmail.com]
Subject: FW: Great Stuff!

Omigod, Sara—*Wait till you read this mail from Jon*!!!!!

Is this unbelievable or what?!!! He is so HOT!

You know I already said YES, but my mom-person will never let me go alone, the oppression situation 'n stuff. Say you'll come with me? I'm dancin on the moon.

Here it is:

From: jon draper [captainJ@ezmail.com]
Date: Thurs, 3 Sept 1998 18:27:20 EST
To: Dulciana Newton [DANcer@ezmail.com]
Subject: Great Stuff!

Couldn't stop checkin you out at the coffee shop. My guys think I'm off the deep end, but is it cool if you wait for me after the game tomorrow, go to the Common Ground? I hope Friday night is on order. Say yes! SOON!

Jon

From: Sara Reichert [enigma22@ezmail.com]
Date: Thurs, 3 Sept 1998 18:43:15 EST
To: Dulciana Newton [DANcer@ezmail.com]
Subject: RE: FW: Great Stuff!

Dulcie

You go, moon child. But me: you gotta be kiddin! I know he's a hottie to you, but no way I'm gonna be a 3rd wheel while the 1st and 2nd wheels drool over each other.

All for you, girl, but not this one. Sorry.

From: Dulciana Newton [DANcer@ezmail.com]
Date: Thurs, 3 Sept 1998 18:49:15 EST
To: Sara Reichert [enigma22@ezmail.com]
Subject: RE: RE: FW: Great Stuff!

Sara, MY BEST BUD always there when something's up,

PLEASE! PLEASE! PLEASE! PLEASE! PLEASE!
PLEASE! PLEASE!

Jon is IT! We really connected! I HAVE to
see him again.

I *promise* I won't drool.

please! please! please! please! please!
please! please!

Holdin my breath,

D

From: Sara Reichert [enigma22@ezmail.com]
Date: Thurs, 3 Sept 1998 18:58:15 EST
To: Dulciana Newton [DANcer@ezmail.com]
Subject: RE: RE: RE: FW: Great Stuff!

OK! OK! Breathe! This is so NUTS. But I'll
do it for you.

From: Dulciana Newton [DANcer@ezmail.com]
Date: Thurs, 3 Sept 1998 19:03:35 EST
To: Sara Reichert [enigma22@ezmail.com]
Subject: RE: RE: RE: RE: FW: Great Stuff!

I won't ever forget. THANK YOU! THANK YOU!
THANK YOU! THANK YOU! THANK YOU! THANK YOU!
THANK YOU! THANK YOU!

Your friend forever,

Dulcie

My Journal, My Life

Thursday Night, September 3, 1998

Monsieur Henri de Toulouse-Lautrec
Café des Artistes
Left Bank
Paris, France

Cher Henri,

Two days of school down and a million to go!

I'm in an Honors English Lit/Creative Writing class this year. Ms. Blake is really good but TOUGH. We'll have tons of reading, and we'll be studying lots of different authors. I hear Ms. Blake is in love with revision. And she wants a hellish amount of work—a paper already by next Friday, then one every three weeks!!! She says that writing is the only way to learn to write. I foresee callused fingers. We're reading Romeo and Juliet *this semester. She really liked my haiku— said it had "honesty."*

Foster child tries, fails,
screams when she's sent back again.
Winter smothers all.

*The rest of school sucks. Worst thing? Dulcie has totally
lost it. Last year, it was us against the Rich Bitches, the
Brains, and the Freaks (except Shawn, who was maybe going
to be my friend until Carol said I couldn't see her anymore.
Just because she has 15 earrings and a couple tattoos and
runs away from home sometimes because of her mother's
boyfriends, she's a "bad influence"?).*

*Now, it's like Dulcie's morphed into some person I don't
even know.*

*She wants to be with these rich girls at lunch! Has she for-
gotten how they used to treat her? I sit with her but I don't
talk to them. Not that they care. Those airheads never talk
about anything but cars, clothes, horses, boys, and football.
Dulcie, of course, HAS to go to every game. Next thing I
know, she'll be trying out for cheerleader. I have nothing to
contribute to any of it.*

In happier news—

*Carol got a scanner! You probably don't know about
those—you put the paper you want to copy in the top, and it
slides down under a roller. Then the scanner copies it into
your PC. You can make it into a picture that you put in a doc-
ument, or you can fax it, or whatever.*

I have to use Carol's PC to scan stuff in, but then I put it up on the server for our network, and I can call it up on my PC screen in my room. It is so great!

Here's the first thing I scanned in—from the "Teen" section in the newspaper. I really like this girl's writing—she has good ideas, writes about important topics like this one on depression. Once you start reading her columns, you can't stop till the end. Ms. Blake says that's what happens when you take time to revise and really polish your writing. Sigh. . . .

I cut and pasted the column to give you the parts I like best. Here it is:

THE HOME DAILY

TEEN / TUESDAY, SEPTEMBER 1, 1998

DEPRESSION—SLOGGING THROUGH SNOWDRIFTS

By Helena Leasor

My aunt Connie—sleepless, thoughts whirling—felt alone and helpless.

She and my uncle Bob, who had not fought in twenty years of marriage, now totally couldn't speak to each other.

A month before, Connie and Bob had driven twelve hundred miles. The two cats complained the whole time.

The nightmare began at the new house—which seemed perfect when they bought it. Three leaks had soaked their bedroom carpet, the cupboard beneath the kitchen sink, and the wall in the guest bath. Frantic calls brought plumber and carpet cleaner.

Trash, an old boat motor, and a broken off-road vehicle littered the garage. Then the movers arrived to unload.

For five days, huge fans whirred in their bedroom, and the cats hid while the people worked nonstop.

Now the house was livable, but city, county, and state red tape was making Bob crazy. Connie, a writer, hadn't written one word.

They had both tried.

They e-mailed and called friends, including me—made the horror stories funny. Bob vented. Connie treated herself—a bubble bath, an iced mocha, a bunch of flowers—every day. She told me she even sobbed in the shower so that Bob wouldn't hear.

Now, with her best friend sleeping next to her, Connie felt as if she were totally alone, slogging through ten-foot snowdrifts.

She got up that night and wrote every ugly, self-defeating thought. She wrote until she was exhausted, then went back to bed and finally slept.

In the morning, she called a therapist.

Experts say that every year, 17.5 million Americans suffer from clinical depression. On average, one person every seventeen minutes commits suicide. It is rated third among the leading causes of death for young people.

Connie and Bob got help. Everyone who is depressed should.

I love that phrase "slogging through ten-foot snowdrifts." I picture that snow crusted with ice.

Won't write tomorrow. Going to the game (I HATE football) with Dulcie, and after, we're meeting The Jock.

Dulcie says he's the best thing that ever happened to her. What about me? Whine, whine.

Good night, Henri. At least I have you.

Love, Sara

P.S. Did you read any Charles Dickens? Here's a paraphrase of some of his words:

> *I only ask to be free. The butterflies are free.*
> *Mankind will surely not deny to Sara Reichert*
> *what it concedes to the butterflies!*

My Journal, My Life

THURSDAY NIGHT, SEPTEMBER 10, 1998

MONSIEUR HENRI DE TOULOUSE-LAUTREC
CAFÉ DES ARTISTES
LEFT BANK
PARIS, FRANCE

Cher Henri,

Too busy to write. Have been slaving over my first paper for Ms. Blake. I'll show you each one, then when I get her critiques, I'll put those in right afterward. Here it is:

HONORS ENGLISH LIT/CREATIVE WRITING
SCENE FOR CONTEMPORARY PLAY
WORKING TITLE: *Coffeehouse*
September 11, 1998

CHARACTERS: Kara (tall, big, baggy clothes), Ashley (short, tiny, yellow shirt), Bob (tall, blond, varsity sweater over cotton sweater), and Joe, the coffeehouse owner.

SCENE: *Common Ground after the game. The decibel level is high—chatter, girls' screams, laughter, jukebox.*

Ashley and Bob walk in holding hands. Kara follows— drooping shoulders, lips tight. Two boys at a table across the room call to Bob. Bob goes over to the table while Ashley and Kara slide into a blue plastic booth and sit across from each other.

ASHLEY: He is so amazing. Isn't he amazing?
KARA: You promised not to drool.
ASHLEY: I'm just so happy! This is me, smiling.

KARA: *(Hands her a napkin.)* Wipe your mouth.

ASHLEY: *(Throws the napkin at Kara.)* I am totally nervous. Does it show?

KARA: You look totally great.

ASHLEY: Do you think he really likes me?

KARA: I think, I think.

ASHLEY: *(Watches Bob across room.)* He is so cute.

KARA: What does cute mean in the big scheme of things?

ASHLEY: But he's funny, too. Don't you think he's funny?

KARA: Do you see me laughing?

ASHLEY: And he's nice. And an amazing quarterback.

KARA: So?

ASHLEY: Tell me you don't love his convertible.

KARA: I don't love his convertible. *(Ashley makes a face.)* Couldn't resist. Okay, it's a nice car.

ASHLEY: Why don't you like him?

KARA: I just don't trust him. I—

BOB: *(Sliding in beside Ashley.)* Tim and Allen had to give me a hard time about having *two* girls.

KARA: And you said?

BOB: That I was the luckiest guy in the room. Said I didn't want them stealing either one of my cool chicks.

KARA: Can you spell *sophomoric*?

BOB: You say that like it's a bad thing.

KARA: Unbelievable. So, what do we want? I'll go get it. I'm having my usual.

ASHLEY: Me too.

BOB: *(Holding out his wallet)* Me three. And I'm buying.

KARA: Thanks. *(She walks to the counter.)* Three usuals, Joe.

JOE: Coming right up. One cappuccino and a tea biscuit for my friend Kara. A latte with skim milk for the too-skinny princess. Flavor of the Day for the quarterback—extra whipped cream, two chocolate-chocolate chip cookies on the side.

(Kara watches Bob and Ashley whisper in the booth, heads together. She sighs and hands Joe the money.)

KARA: *(Back at the table.)* Bob, your wallet. Ashley, want half? Hey! Is anybody in there?

ASHLEY: No sweets for me, remember?

KARA: Joe says you're too skinny.

BOB: I say she's perfect. Let me put that data into my hold file, along with all the other stuff you've told me. Two parents—adopted. Two cats—also adopted. Two sisters. Loves to swim, hates sitcoms, loves animals, doesn't get jazz—

KARA: I didn't know that.

BOB: *(Goes on.)* Doesn't eat sweets. *(Drapes an arm over Ashley's shoulder, peers into her face.)* Eyes? The color of dark chocolate.

ASHLEY: *(Drops her eyes, smiles, sighs.)*

KARA: You're just a little computer, Bob, aren't you? You spit out facts.

BOB: *(Touches Ashley's hair.)* When it comes to someone I care about.

KARA: So. What about you, Bob? Tell us.

BOB: The usual—two parents, one brother, one dog, love old westerns, hate stupid people, love all kinds of music as long as it has good lyrics.

KARA: I suppose you like poetry, too?

BOB: Well . . .

ASHLEY: Me neither, if I don't understand it.

BOB: Favorite color—yellow. Favorite movie—*Clerks.* *(Waves when a couple girls call his name as they leave.)*

KARA: *(Watches Ashley's face.)* You are Mr. Popularity, aren't you, Bob?

BOB: C'mon. They're my buds. You'll like them.

ASHLEY: Everybody knows the quarterback, Kara. *(Smiles at Bob; moves a little closer.)* Especially one who wins games.

BOB: You got it.

KARA: Talk about your giant egos.

BOB: Just kidding, Kara. Tell me about you.

KARA: Oh, please! Don't bother opening up another data file. There's nothing to tell. You don't want to hear about me. You can tell him, Ashley.

ASHLEY: Kara's my best friend. She's loyal, smart, kind—

KARA: Hey, I meant later. And don't make me sound like a golden retriever, okay? I'll just finish up here, then take off.

BOB: You will NOT. *(Bob spills his coffee.)*

KARA: Whoa. Run for high ground. *(Scrambles out of the booth.)*

(Joe tosses Bob a towel. The towel lands on his face instead of his outstretched hands, and he claps his hands in front of his face, pretends to be shot.)

KARA: *(Laughs.)* Omigod, the boy can't catch.

BOB: *(As he and Ashley mop up the spill.)* I did that on purpose, you know. Perfect people are so hard to live with.

KARA: *(Laughs.)* As if . . . Stop it, Bob. You'll make me get the hiccups.

ASHLEY: She does that if she laughs too much.

BOB: Okay, okay. Where was I? Oh yeah. Kara, you can't go home alone.

KARA: Why not?

BOB: I told my buds I'd skip going back to Allen's place for brews tonight, 'cause I had to take BOTH my girls home. *(Leans closer.)* Say okay, okay?

KARA: *(Hiccups.)* You are too much.

CRITIQUE FROM CLARISSA BLAKE:

Sara,

I like <u>Coffeehouse</u> a lot. Dialogue is crisp and natural. You have created two strong characters in Kara and Bob, and it would be fun for teen actors to play them.

About Ashley, however: She could almost not be there, except as the catalyst for Kara and Bob. In order to make this a well-rounded three-character play, you need to give Ashley more to do, more that will let us see her as a person instead of an object.

The Drama Club is always looking for short plays. Think about it.

My Journal, My Life

Cher Henri,

Late this morning, because of that stupid train. And because of Carol—she poked and prodded—trying to get me to talk.

I listened. She said I looked like a slob. She asked why I don't dress like Dulcie. Next she'll tell me I should wear PINK NAIL POLISH.

She did find me a couple of big soft Henley tees at a garage sale—one in rust and one in dark green—and I let her know I like them.

Why do people always want to change their kids?

Now, whether to ask Carol that? I think not.

It is totally hectic around here. You can't imagine how much reading AND WRITING I have to do for Ms. Blake's Lit class. So I'm doing it. She says my stuff has "raw power." How about that?!

Dulcie and I are reading Catcher in the Rye, *which was written back in 1951. How can anything so old be SO like the way life is now? When I'm reading the book, I AM Holden Caulfield. We both cried when Holden explained the title.*

Thank God Ms. Blake doesn't make us read our papers out loud in class unless we want to. That would be the death of my writing, at least my honest, raw-power writing. This is the first class ever where I want to be the best.

Went to see a movie with Dulcie, Jon, Ted, and Anthony. Seems like the only way to spend time with Dulcie anymore is to spend time with Jon and his guys. At least the theater has fabulous buttered popcorn.

A discovery: Jon is not only a jock (although I don't think anyone would ever accuse him of being a genius). He's an independent- and Japanese-film freak. Seen every Akira Kurosawa film. So how can anybody whose favorite movie is Clerks *be all bad? And he absolutely loves sushi, which I plan to try someday. Or maybe not.*

I'm a little worried about Dulcie because I heard that Jon drinks. Only beer, and he's not an alcoholic or anything but still. . . . At the hospital, that time I took the pills, they said that drinking is really bad if you're depressed or angry. I don't think Dulcie ever drinks, and those two are so totally far from depressed or angry, they're balloons floating on air. So I don't know—it's probably all right.

Almost forgot. A really weird nightmare thing happened right in the middle of the movie.

We're all laughing at something on the screen—I'm next to Ted—and his leg touches mine. And it doesn't move away.

Suddenly I'm paralyzed in a cold dark cave, our legs the only thing in the world. My chin quivers and—this is so stupid—I have to fight back tears. I make a fist to hit Ted, but stop myself, and it's like moving a three-ton boulder, but, finally, I drag myself away.

I stumble out the other end of the row, and by the time I make it to the ladies' room, I'm snuffling and choking like a baby.

Man! Can you spell overreaction?

Your friend, Sara

P.S. This fits my mood:

> *So we beat on, boats against the current, borne back ceaselessly into the past.*
>
> *—F. Scott Fitzgerald*

From: Sara Reichert [enigma22@ezmail.com]
Date: Mon, 14 Sept 1998 22:16:54 EST
To: Dulciana Newton [DANcer@ezmail.com]
Subject: Ranting

Dulcie,

How can you stand it? Those girls are
RIDICULOUS! Trish hates her parents because
her palomino isn't challenging enuf and
they won't get her a new horse? Heather has
to be excused from school in November so
that she can go ski in Austria?

Ted and Anthony are okay, but the rest of
that crowd is so totally clueless.

Please. Can we change something? Could we
at least not eat lunch with them?

Sara

From: Dulciana Newton [DANcer@ezmail.com]
Date: Mon, 14 Sept 1998 23:10:15 EST
To: Sara Reichert [enigma22@ezmail.com]
Subject: RE: Ranting

Sara,

You're not giving them a chance. I know Heather's a brat, but Trish's nice. She asked me this morning where I got my sweater, and when I told her, she offered to take me with her to New York next time. Why would she do that if she wasn't a nice person?

I refuse to hate people just because they're different from me. You should understand that.

And they're Jon's friends. He has to spend time with them because all their parent-peeps hang out together, go to the same dances, work on the same benefits 'n stuff. He can't help who his friends are.

Dulcie

From: Sara Reichert [enigma22@ezmail.com]
Date: Mon, 14 Sept 1998 23:26:54 EST
To: Dulciana Newton [DANcer@ezmail.com]
Subject: RE: RE: Ranting

Dulcie,

Of course he can help who his friends are.
And these're all so stupid! Okay, Jon's
different, but how can HE stand it? They
don't know anything about what the real
world's like. I mean, how many yachts can
you use at one time?

Do any of them own anything without quotes
around it? A "cottage" (with a spa and
cathedral ceilings) at the lake. A "farm"
(that no food grows on) in Hunting Meadows.
An "apartment" (with 20 rooms) in New York.
Please! Talk about "pretentious"!

Sara

From: Dulciana Newton [DANcer@ezmail.com]
Date: Mon, 14 Sept 1998 23:30:19 EST
To: Sara Reichert [enigma22@ezmail.com]
Subject: RE: RE: RE: Ranting

Sara, just give them a chance. Talk to them.
They'll be nice to you too. Say you'll try.

D

From: Sara Reichert [enigma22@ezmail.com]
Date: Mon, 14 Sept 1998 23:46:54 EST
To: Dulciana Newton [DANcer@ezmail.com]
Subject: RE: RE: RE: RE: Ranting

I won't, Dulcie. Don't you see? These are
NOT nice people. If they ever even look
like they might be nice to me, I'll run the
other way.

S

From: Dulciana Newton [DANcer@ezmail.com]
Date: Mon, 14 Sept 1998 23:56:15 EST
To: Sara Reichert [enigma22@ezmail.com]
Subject: RE: RE: RE: RE: RE: Ranting

Sara, you're wrong. Don't want to discuss
it anymore. See you in the AM.

D

From: Sara Reichert [enigma22@ezmail.com]
Date: Tues, 15 Sept 1998 00:13:54 EST
To: Dulciana Newton [DANcer@ezmail.com]
Subject: RE: RE: RE: RE: RE: RE: Ranting

Dulcie,

One more tiny thing—you know I have to have
the last word.

Please, just THINK about this:

<<. . . *love does not consist in gazing at
each other but in looking together in the
same direction.*>>

                    —Antoine de Saint-Exupéry

45

What do I know, but I think that quote means if you and Jon spend all your time looking into each other's eyes, you can't see what's really happening around you.

Love, Sara

My Journal, My Life

Tuesday Night, September 15, 1998
Monsieur Henri de Toulouse-Lautrec
Paris, France

Mon Cher Monsieur Henri,

Things are getting complicated. It started this morning when I forgot my Soc book.

Dulcie goes on to class, I'm wading through my locker, and I hear this guy say, "Hey, Jon! I hear that Oriental stuff is HOT. You burn yourself yet?"

Big laugh!

Then some girl's voice: "She said she'd love to ride, but she doesn't have a horse."

Another big laugh. Another girl's voice: "So why doesn't she just get one?"

I slam my locker door and whirl around, but they're gone.

I HAVE to do something. Help me figure out what, okay?

I could just stick it out, hang with those rich bitches until Dulcie gets hurt and finally sees what they're like. Like that is so not going to happen!

I can keep badgering Dulcie. Sure! And then she ends up hating me.

I could say something to one of THEM. I don't care what they think of me, but they might just hurt Dulcie more. And they're still going to be Jon's friends.

I don't think Jon gets it. Do guys ever get it?

I could tell him what's going on, and he could stop it. Or, if he's not serious about Dulcie, he could break up with her before anything more happens.

But what if he breaks up with Dulcie, and she finds out it's because of me?

How would she find out?

She wouldn't.

Okay. Thanks, Henri.

To be continued.

Love, Sara

From: Sara Reichert [enigma22@ezmail.com]
Date: Tues, 15 Sept 1998 23:16:54 EST
To: jon draper [captainJ@ezmail.com]
Subject: Dulcie

Jon,

We're not exactly friends yet, so you'll probably think this is none of my business, but IT IS. Because Dulcie is my friend.

Do you realize how much you're hurting her, putting her in with that coven of witches? They're laughing at her behind her back. They'll never accept her, because she's not one of them. I don't care, but SHE does.

If you're serious about Dulcie, you have to tell your peeps, get them to back off.

Or, if you're not, if your friends mean more to you than Dulcie does, you have to break up with her now, before she really gets hurt.

She won't listen to me, but she will to
you.

Please do something before it's too late.

Sara

My Journal, My Life

SEPTEMBER 15, 1998

Cher Henri,

I'm so SCARED. Fingers are like ice chunks. Can hardly type. Sent the email to Jon. Either smartest thing I ever did, or the stupidest.

Love, Sara

From: Dulciana Newton [DANcer@ezmail.com]
Date: Wed, 16 Sept 1998 20:10:15 EST
To: Sara Reichert [enigma22@ezmail.com]
Subject: Jon

Jon forwarded your letter. Thank you very
much! How could you? I thought you were my
friend. Just so you know—Jon is NOT break-
ing up with me.

Please don't interfere in my life anymore.

Dulcie

From: Sara Reichert [enigma22@ezmail.com]
Date: Wed, 16 Sept 1998 20:16:54 EST
To: Dulciana Newton [DANcer@ezmail.com]
Subject: RE: Jon

Dulcie,

You don't understand. I AM your friend.
That's why I did it. Can't we talk about it?

Sara

My Journal, My Life

SEPTEMBER 16, 1998 11:30 P.M.

Cher Henri,

Oh, God. No mail from Dulcie. She won't answer mine, or come to the phone.

It's like my sister, Susie. When I told the Children's Services woman about Daddy, I was trying to save Susie, but they took her away. Daddy put his fist through the door, drank a whole bottle of booze, and snored for a week, while Mama cried.

Why did Jon do that? There was no reason for him to send her my mail. Now I've done exactly what I was trying to keep from happening—hurt Dulcie.

Susie didn't know me when I saw her again last year. Her new mom and dad tried to help but . . .

What if Dulcie never speaks to me again?

What should I do?

Oh, God, this is awful. I'm so tired.

Good night, Henri.

Sara

My Journal, My Life

SEPTEMBER 17, 1998

Cher Henri,

Rained all day today—inside and out.

Dulcie still not speaking. Saw her at lunchtime, holding hands with Jon, getting into his car. She wouldn't even look at me.

What am I going to do? I have a headache I'm so mad, and I'm not sure who with. Jon? Dulcie? Me?

Had that nightmare again last night. In the dream I fight and fight and can't get away, and I'm hitting as hard as I can, but I think I should be able to hit harder. Then the person puts something over my face, I can't breathe, everything goes black.

I wake up and I'm hitting Carol. I let her hold me for a little. She gets me a drink, and puts some music on.

Then, today, thanks to Hannah, I'm in trouble with Carol. I take a shower, and afterward my ankh (it's silver, and a symbol that means enduring life) is gone from my dresser top. Dulcie gave me the ankh at Christmas last year, and I've worn it around my neck, on a leather thong, every day since.

I know Hannah's the one who stole it.

Of course I immediately go to her room. And, of course, she stares at me like I'm speaking Latin, then screams, "I did not! Get out of here!" and bursts into tears.

And, of course, Carol takes her side. "What makes you think Hannah took it?" she asks me.

"Look at her," I say, as calm as I can make myself. "You know how she is when she's done something. Her face is red as a tomato."

Carol says, "She's been crying." She turns to Hannah and says softly, "Did you take Sara's ankh?"

Hannah screams at me, "I hate you!" and runs out of the room.

"She's a little girl," Carol says, "not a hardened criminal. I'm sorry your ankh is lost, but it seems to me you could give Hannah a break once in a while."

What could I do? I say, "I'm sorry," and look out the window. She's obviously so disappointed in me.

Whatever. I'll take care of this my own way.

Well, Henri, if I can focus, instead of thinking about this mess called my life, it's time to study. I'll try to talk to Dulcie again tomorrow. She HAS to listen to me. I'll do whatever it takes.

Night.

Sara

P.S. I sent this to Dulcie. Not a word from her!

There is no greater sorrow than to recall a time of happiness in misery.

—Dante

From: Dulciana Newton [DANcer@ezmail.com]
Date: Fri, 18 Sept 1998 17:10:15 EST
To: Sara Reichert [enigma22@ezmail.com]
Subject: Forgive me please?

Hey Sara!

How could I be so stupid? I am SO SORRY I doubted you. Why did it take me so long to figure this out?

Jon reminded me about how nasty those kids were last year before YOU stopped them.

And YOU WERE RIGHT! Something happened, Jon won't say what, but he doesn't want to hang with those rich kids anymore. The reason Anthony and Ted are different is cause they've known Jon since sixth grade. They're poor, too, like us. Well, not poor, but you know what I mean—monetarily challenged.

So, can you forgive me, please? Are we still friends?

Love, Dulcie

From: Sara Reichert [enigma22@ezmail.com]
Date: Fri, 18 Sept 1998 17:16:54 EST
To: Dulciana Newton [DANcer@ezmail.com]
Subject: RE: Forgive me please?

Dulcie,

We are! I am SO HAPPY!

Want to come over? Carol rented a movie I
don't want to see, but she's making popcorn. We could just hang out for a while.

From: Dulciana Newton [DANcer@ezmail.com]
Date: Fri, 18 Sept 1998 17:20:15 EST
To: Sara Reichert [enigma22@ezmail.com]
Subject: RE: RE: Forgive me please?

:) See you in 5.

My Journal, My Life

September 18, 1998

Cher Henri,

Fabulous news. Last week Carol said I could drive her new car. It's called a Beetle, and I guess the old ones are from way back in the '70s, but now they're making them again. It's really cute and I even get to take it to school sometimes. Of course, there's always a catch. You'll see what that is in this scene I turned in today for H Eng homework. It's based on a scene from The Giver *(which we read last week), so it's kind of over the top, but. . . .*

HONORS ENGLISH LIT/CREATIVE WRITING
SHORT SCENE FROM MY LIFE
IN THE STYLE OF LOIS LOWRY,
INSPIRED BY *The Giver*
900 Words
September 18, 1998

Susanna and Kenny, scattering pigeons, ran to Darra when she pulled into the lot at Edgewater Park. Darra's mind shut out the previous excitement of driving the new Beetle for the first time on her own; she felt anxious and irritated.

"Hurry up!" the kids said, and dragged her by both hands to where Meryl sat on a blanket, the picnic spread out around her on the bank overlooking the lake and city skyline.

Meryl waited until the children plopped down. Then she spoke. "I know," she said in her dynamic, refined voice, "that you feel I'm being ridiculously mysterious."

She smiled. "I've worried you," she said, "and I'm sorry."

Susanna said, "Are you sick, Mom?"

"Did I do something?" Kenny leaned up close to Meryl.

"I'm fine," Meryl said with a smile, "and no one did anything wrong." She looked at Darra. "I especially apologize to you. You haven't been with us for long."

"It's okay," Darra mumbled. She wasn't used to anyone apologizing to her.

"I need help from all of you," Meryl said, "especially Darra. Beginning next week, I'm going to start studying for my MCSE tests, some computer certifications I need for my business."

"What's that mean?" Kenny said. "I'm starving. Can I open the chips?"

Meryl ruffled his hair. "Go ahead. What I'll be doing is like going to school in my office at home. I'll need time and quiet because this is really hard stuff. Understand?"

"But what about Girl Scouts?" Susanna said. "And my skating? You are coming, aren't you?"

"Now, honey," Meryl said. "Would I ever miss the finals?"

Susanna smiled.

Kenny crunched a chip.

Meryl got to her feet. "Please come here, Darra."

Darra willed herself to move heavy feet, to stand next to Meryl. She felt Meryl's arm across her tense shoulders.

"Give me my car keys, please."

Darra's heart sank as she pulled them from her pocket.

"You all know how much I depend on my truck for my business," Meryl went on. "It's like my second office."

They all nodded. They were forbidden to touch anything in it.

"And you know I love our new car."

They nodded again. They wiped the dew off the car every morning before leaving for school. They clapped their heels together to clean their shoes before getting in.

In a commanding voice, Meryl announced, "From now on, Darra will be Second-in-Command at our house."

Darra blinked. What did that mean?

Susanna picked at a thread in her sweater. Kenny, a chip halfway to his mouth, looked from his mom to Darra.

Meryl went on in a lighter tone. "I've observed Darra since she came to live with us. She has all the qualities necessary."

For what?

With her hand still firmly on Darra's shoulder, Meryl listed the qualities.

"Intelligence," she said. "We're all aware that Darra's school grades are good and getting better.

"Integrity," she said, and smiled. "Darra has, like all of us, committed minor transgressions. I expect that.

She has always let me know when she's done something wrong.

"Courage," she went on. "Only I, in our family, have ever undergone the difficulties of driving with more than one child. And of studying with children in the house." She smiled at Susanna and Kenny.

A seagull swooped low over the cliff.

"Darra," she said, "I'm putting my children in your hands."

Darra felt fear flutter within her, saw Kenny's frown of concentration.

"No!" Susanna looked stricken.

Meryl lifted a hand. "You know I love my children more than life. They are my memories of Tom, my reasons to go on."

Darra nodded, remembering Meryl's concern about every scrape and bruise, every least slight experienced by either of them at school.

Meryl went on. "If anything happens to either of these children, you will be faced with pain that you cannot understand now. I cannot prepare you for that. But I know that you are brave."

Darra did not feel brave at that moment.

"The fourth essential quality," Meryl said, "is wisdom. You don't have that yet. But I know you have the ability to acquire it. Can you do this, Darra?"

Darra looked at Susanna and Kenny, and tenderness for them grew inside her, as if they were a real sister and brother. She remembered fighting for her own sister, Susie, when she was little, protecting her from Daddy.

She straightened slightly. Briefly she felt a sliver of sureness. "I can do it," she said.

"Good!" Meryl squeezed Darra's shoulder, and handed her keys that dangled from a blue and gold butterfly. "These are your keys to the car and to the house. Thank you for accepting this tremendous responsibility."

Then she sat down and began removing the plastic wrap from the sandwiches. Susanna and Kenny chanted, "Darra," low at first, barely a murmur, then louder, "DARRA, DARRA, DARRA."

With that, Darra knew that the kids accepted her in her new role in their family.

Her heart swelled with gratitude and pride, but at the same time she was scared. What did this really mean?

Darra dropped the keys into her pocket, and, as they ate, her fingers jingled them often.

So, Henri, what do you think? I know it's melodramatic, and, of course, I fictionalized it.

The real thing wasn't that scary, and what Carol really said to me was, "Now you're the real Big Sister in the family. And with freedom comes responsibility." What she means is I can use the car now, but (and this is a big BUT) I am also

*responsible for carting the kids around when she can't do it.
Oh, well. . . . I can do this, right?*

*Oh, and—surprise, surprise—the kids did NOT chant my
name like they did in* The Giver. *But they did say, "Okay."*

Good night, my friend.

Sara

*P.S. Thought football players weren't supposed to drink.
Shows you what I know. Dulcie says they all do.*

*All you need in this life is ignorance and confidence;
then success is sure.*

—*Mark Twain*

CRITIQUE FROM CLARISSA BLAKE:

Sara,

An A- on your scene. I could tell you chose the scene from <u>The Giver</u> where Jonas is given his mission as the new receiver. How wonderful you must have felt when "Meryl" gave you that responsibility.

You showed interaction among people, and gave us conflict even though it was only "Darra" with herself. You gave us a snapshot of the environment, a moment in time. Your characters moved physically, and you gave us facial expressions, voice, and emotions. You stayed in single-character point of view. But—you knew there would be one, didn't you?—next time, give us less talk and more action.

My Journal, My Life

WEDNESDAY NIGHT, SEPTEMBER 30, 1998

Cher Henri,

Apologies for not having written for more than a week. So much has happened.

This next article is also from the "Teen" section. It'll help explain what I've been doing.

THE HOME DAILY
TEEN / TUESDAY, SEPTEMBER 29, 1998

TEEN CLASSICAL EVENING PROMOTES AWARENESS OF SEXUAL ABUSE
By Tonie Vend

Westview High School is going classical for an evening. Think *Aida,* satin dresses, tuxes, and exotic desserts. For sure, no one will be wearing rock-band T-shirts to the school's annual benefit for the Rape,

Abuse & Incest National Network (RAINN) on October 7.

RAINN is a nonprofit organization based in Washington, D.C. Founded in 1994, the organization operates a national toll-free hot line (1–800–555–HOPE) for survivors of sexual abuse. Proceeds from this year's concert will go toward keeping the hot line open.

"A Night at the Opera," presented in conjunction with the school's National Honor Society chapter, will feature Westview students, faculty, and alumni, as well as guest musicians from Baldwin-Wallace and Oberlin Colleges. Among those scheduled to perform are Westview High junior Dulcie Newton who will sing an original song, accompanied on guitar by herself and music teacher Janet Stevens.

"Last year we had a rap concert, which raised over $1,000," says Westview guidance counselor Joe P. Daly. "This year's goal is $1,500."

Jon Draper, 17, a senior and the football quarterback, came up with the idea for the fund-raiser. "I thought it was important to raise awareness about sexual abuse. And a national hot-line number is the quickest help in today's mobile society."

This year, Draper was named national student coordinator for RAINN. He helps high schools across the country develop promotional events and fund-raisers for the organization.

FOR YOUR INFORMATION:

"A Night at the Opera" will be held at 7 P.M., October 7, at Westview High School, 4507 Middleton Road. Tickets are $10 for adults, $5 for students. Tickets may be purchased in advance at the guidance office.

So what do you think, Henri? Is this super or what? How can anyone not like Jon?? Or is he too good to be true? I mean, he still doesn't have a clue about the real world, but he sure knows how to get stuff done.

I'm so proud of Dulcie. And they talked me into being the decorations chairman! We're going to have streamers of football mums hanging from the ceiling like Egyptian columns. The principal said not to even think about real animals (like they have in the opera), so I talked to the art classes and they're making papier-mâché life-size animals, like camels and elephants. It's going to be fabulous. I never knew that doing stuff like this for other people could be fun.

And more good news. I asked Carol if I could redo my room and she said YES! She even apologized, said she forgot it wasn't a guest room anymore. Good-bye, pink-and-blue bedspread. No more wedding picture of Carol's mother and father, or baby pictures of Hannah and Keith. Farewell to that wreath of dried baby's breath on the door. Maybe I'll paint the walls black.

We're going shopping next weekend. All I have to do to pay for it is rake the leaves. "All," she says. That's the leaves from forty trees! I am going to be so buff by Christmas!

Sara

P.S. Have you heard of "Udder Cream"? Farmers use it for their cows, but it's great for the callus on my raking hand.

P.P.S. I've discovered that when Jon gets excited about any-thing—and I mean ANYthing—he spills his coffee. I try to always sit where I can leap up when that coffee comes at me. Isn't it amazing? The guy has a flaw.

P.P.P.S. How could I forget? Am reading Maya Angelou. Talk about honest and raw power. She is fabulous. And I may not be an African-American girl but I, too, "know why the caged bird sings."

P.P.P.P.S. Here's the story I'm turning in on Friday.

HONORS ENGLISH LIT/CREATIVE WRITING
OBJECTIVE NARRATION—IN THE STYLE OF
ERNEST HEMINGWAY,
INSPIRED BY *Hills Like White Elephants*
October 2, 1998

Gulls Like Crying Cats

The waters of Lake Erie, north of Cleveland, were blue, ruffled, and sprinkled with whitecaps. Over the water, seagulls swooped, dove, and called.

A railroad bridge spanned the Cuyahoga River just before it emptied into the lake. On the shore, a restaurant was laid out on a pier next to the track. Outside the building sat white plastic tables with umbrellas and chairs. The many-colored flags along the pier whipped in the wind. The girl and the woman with her sat at an outside table in the shade of an umbrella near the bar.

"When does Dad get off work?" the girl asked.

The woman looked at her watch. "In about an hour. He'll want to leave here right away."

The girl had slipped her feet from her sandals and propped them on the metal base of the table.

The woman fanned herself with a menu. "This darn humidity!" she said. "Wouldn't you rather be inside in the air-conditioning?"

"I like it outside."

"It's too hot to eat," the woman said.

"Let's get iced coffees."

"I think twelve is a bit young for coffee, but for once, I guess. . . . Two iced lattes," the woman called to the bartender.

"Cinnamon or nutmeg on top?" the man asked.

"Cinnamon on both."

The bartender brought two cups and two napkins. He put the napkins and the cups on the table and left.

The girl looked off at the expanse of lake visible beneath the span of the black iron railroad bridge. It was dotted with white foam in the sun, and seagulls perched on the bridge.

"The gulls sound like kittens crying, don't they, Mom?" she said.

"Not to me," the woman said, and sipped her coffee.

The girl shrugged and looked up at the gulls.

"They're so beautiful," she said, "but now they sound like angry cats."

"Dad told you last night that it's not your fault, Jen. But it's not *my* fault either. It's no one's fault."

The girl wet a finger and rubbed at a coffee stain on the tabletop.

"I know it'll be better for you this way. You know you haven't been happy with us."

The girl did not say anything.

"Dad and I will go inside with you, and stay while you get unpacked and settled."

"Then what?"

"You'll be fine. It won't be long until you're in the right place."

The girl looked at her blue-striped toenails, leaned down and flicked an ant off her foot.

"Yeah. There'll probably be hundreds of couples hanging around waiting for me."

"There are many childless couples. You don't have to be afraid. This happens with lots of kids."

"Yeah, I've known some. They were wacko."

"Well," the woman said, and hesitated, "if you don't want to go back right away today, I guess you don't have to. But the arrangements are all made."

"So you really want me to go now?"

"It's for the best. I just can't talk about it anymore. You know this is very hard for me."

"Then I'll do it."

"I don't want you to do it if you feel that way."

The girl stood up and leaned on the railing. A yacht tied up to the dock bobbed in the wake of a passing freighter. Across, on the other shore of the Cuyahoga, were factories, warehouse buildings, a mountain of sand, a marina along the bank, and farther back, the renovated water tower. Far away, the sun was beginning to fall toward the lake.

"I wonder if anybody is ever happy," the girl said.

"Of course. Everybody can be happy."

"Not me."

"Don't say that," the woman said. "You mustn't feel that way."

"I feel how I feel," the girl said.

"I don't want you to do this if you don't want to—"

"I know. Or if it will make me unhappy. Can we just stop talking?"

"If that's what you want."

The girl sat at the table and looked at the bobbing yacht. Its name was painted on the rear—*Serenity.*

The woman didn't say anything but looked at the girl's backpack. It was covered with tin buttons the girl had collected during the five weeks and three days she'd lived with them.

"Dad should be here by now," the woman said. "I'll just go and see if he's out front."

The woman looked up the street, breathing deeply. A long train was passing on the track to her left next to the restaurant. Coming back, she walked slowly through

the tables of people, stopped at the outside bar to pay
the bill, and looked at the girl who was watching a gull
pick up crumbs on the deck.

"Are you ready? Let's wait for Dad out front."

The girl did not say anything, but picked up her
backpack.

"I know this is for the best," the woman said. "Are
you okay?"

"I'm fine," the girl said. "What could be wrong?"

THE END

CRITIQUE FROM CLARISSA BLAKE:

Sara,

Very well done. A definite A+.

You've captured Hemingway's spare prose style beautifully. And you've created a poignant situation for your characters to live through, just as Hemingway did. I ached for that girl, and even a tiny bit for the woman. Isn't it amazing what you can create without "window dressing"?

One suggestion (and I'd make the same one to Mr. Hemingway if he'd listen or were alive): I'd like to see you tighten the description in the opening and in the long paragraph in the middle where the girl stands up to lean on the railing.

Please understand—I don't give this kind of criticism unless I'm looking at good writing. As I've said so often, there is no piece of writing that can't be made better by revision.

I'd like to talk to you about this story. Come see me after classes, okay?

From: Dulciana Newton [DANcer@ezmail.com]
Date: Tues, 6 Oct 1998 22:10:15 EST
To: Sara Reichert [enigma22@ezmail.com]
Subject: Tomorrow night

Pick you up tomorrow night for the RAINN
concert. You'll sit with Ted and Anthony
down front, right? Wanna see all my buds
when I'm singin.

From: Sara Reichert [enigma22@ezmail.com]
Date: Tues, 6 Oct 1998 22:26:54 EST
To: Dulciana Newton [DANcer@ezmail.com]
Subject: RE: Tomorrow night

Bet on it. We'll all be there, stompin and
screamin. Don't come any earlier than 5,
okay? Have to stop in to see Ms. Blake, then
pick up Hannah from SK8 practice at 4:30.
See ya tomorrow night.

My Journal, My Life

WEDNESDAY NIGHT, OCTOBER 7

Cher Henri,

Everybody loved the RAINN concert. And lots of people said the decorations were fabulous. Dulcie looked like a star on Oscar night—red spaghetti-strap dress and (my suggestion) red clunky sandals.

She was FABULOUS—both her singing and accompaniment on the guitar. When she and Ms. Stevens finished, Jon gave each of them a bunch of flowers like they do at the Olympics. Dulcie's song was about belonging, and she got a standing ovation. It was like everybody knew what it feels like to be an outsider. Weird!

Worked at the dessert table, talked with everybody except Trish & Co., who didn't come near me anyway. What a shame they missed Dulcie's mom's apple strudel.

By the way, went to see Ms. Blake after school yesterday. Note on her door said, "Sorry. Family Emergency." Rumor has it her oldest kid is in trouble. Wonder what that's about?

Anyway, don't really want to talk to her about my writing. Maybe she'll forget.

Got to run.

Sara

P.S. Oh, yeah. Got up and boogied in the aisles with Ted and Anthony when the Crazy Men band played at the concert. Did not wear my boots. Don't want to talk about it.

Ted asked if I'd go to a swing club with him some day. I said I can't dance. He said they teach you. I said I'd think about it.

If one touch of his leg brought on that weird reaction, wonder what his hands on my back would bring?

HONORS ENGLISH LIT/CREATIVE WRITING
CHARACTER SKETCHES FOR SHORT STORY
CHARACTERS IN CONFLICT
OCTOBER 9, 1998
First-term Assignment

<u>Point-of-View Character</u>:

<u>Amy Fortier, 15</u>

<u>School</u>

In first grade, cursed a lot, couldn't sit still or keep from shouting out in class.

The teacher called her parents. They wouldn't talk with her, so the teacher called a social worker who made a surprise visit to the Fortier home. The police took Amy and Michael away from the family that day, for the first time.

<u>Amy's family</u>:

<u>Mother</u>—drinks too much, too often, never wanted anything to do with Amy or brother.

<u>Brother</u>—Michael, retarded.

<u>Father</u>—sexually abused Amy and Michael when they were young. Also allowed his brother and his friend with red eyes and goat beard to abuse Amy.

<u>Foster Mother</u>—Betty, see sketch that follows.

<u>Amy's Pain</u>

She doesn't talk about it.

Sometimes blames father. Lashes out in anger at whoever's around.

Sometimes blames self.

In the past, turned pain inward. Burned self with cigarettes and cut self with razor blades—cathartic.

Amy friends with Teri. Betty says Teri has serious problems, forbids Amy to spend time with her.

Amy has been to a therapist who said she has PTSD (Post-traumatic Stress Disorder): recurring dreams, wakes up screaming, "flashbacks" (like when something perfectly normal happens but Amy reacts as if it's something else, something horrible). Example: After Amy helped work on Betty's car, Betty's brother, Uncle Max, hugged Amy. The sweet smell of Uncle Max's after-shave brought on the PTSD: In a second, it turned into her father's sour breath. Amy held herself perfectly still, swallowed a scream, and backed away from Uncle Max.

<u>Beliefs</u>

All 500 boys at her school want to go out with same 10 anorexic girls.

No guy is looking for a normal-size girl who loves
    Scrabble.
People don't care much about one another.
Real love is only in books and movies.
No one will ever love her.
There is never a good reason for war.
Once she's found a family and a friend, she'll be happy.

Second Character:
Teri Jankowski, 15
Doesn't believe she really exists.
If she does, she will not live to be 25.
In case she does, she is cool,
    always wears torn black jeans,
    high-top black sneakers,
    black T-shirts with messages printed on them:

    LIFE IS A FOUR-LETTER WORD.
    LIFE'S A BITCH AND THEN YOU DIE.
    HOW CAN SLAVERY STILL BE LEGAL IN OUR WORLD?
    LET THE DALAI LAMA GO HOME.

Nose ring, eight earrings,
    demons and rams (for Aries, her astrological sign),
    a tattoo of a black rose on her right upper arm,
    black fingernail polish.
Worries constantly:
    about the killings in Rwanda, Bosnia, Algeria,

that the rain forest will disappear,
that Rodney King will be beaten again,
that homelessness will continue to increase until we
all have to live on the streets.

Beliefs

Kids' anthem for the nineties is "Acid, Booze, and
Gangsta Rap."

The Millennium is a time for lunatics to leave the
asylums.

Third Character:
Betty Marchand, 37
Divorced.
Mother of two kids:
Justin, 6,
Heather, 12.
Foster mom of Amy.
Talker and listener:
Tells her kids what's going on in her life and expects
to hear what's going on in theirs.
Talks about how she feels, and wants them to tell her
how they feel, even if how they feel is ugly.
Hard worker. Has own business. Studies hard to
improve skills.
Inclusive:
Makes sure Amy takes part in all family activities,
family meetings, outings. Helps her with home-
work, etc. Goes to every event the school puts on,

especially if one of her kids has a part in the play, pageant, game, etc.

Loves ritual:

Catholic Mass every Sunday.

Does the same things every year for Christmas— whole family does carols at midnight mass on Christmas Eve, gift opening on Christmas morning, then Meals on Wheels for the elderly.

On kids' birthdays (including Amy's) bakes their favorite cake; each kid gets to do what he wants all day long.

Every summer, packs picnics to take to the Metroparks or Holden Arboretum with the kids.

Every winter, organizes sledding trips to the Cuyahoga Valley.

Beliefs

Families should do things together.

Every member of the family should get close to every other member.

If you want privacy, you'll get plenty of it in the grave.

Everyone must work.

CRITIQUE FROM CLARISSA BLAKE:

Sara,

Although, as you know, this is an ungraded exercise, I must tell you that you have created three interesting characters in conflict. You are a long way into an excellent short story for next semester.

Keep it up. Can't wait to see the story.

Also, my apologies again for missing our appointment. As I said when we talked, only an emergency could have kept me from being there.

My Journal, My Life

Cher Henri,

Guess what? I made the Honor Society! Me! Sara Reichert—foster kid from southern Ohio with the bad attitude—made the Honor Society. Who woulda thunk it? Wow! Carol said she wasn't surprised.

And, I'm almost afraid to say it, but I have to tell you—Jon, Dulcie, Ted, and Anthony are all my friends now. Spending lots of time together, and the more I find out about the guys, even Jon, the more I like them. They're guys, but they don't hit on me. They treat me like a bud, not a girl. Jon does really care about Dulcie—he's always giving her something. Like today he gave her his copy of an early Calvin and Hobbes book that he's had since he was a kid. And last week he gave her ten pounds of sunflower hearts because he found out she likes to feed the birds.

Sometimes Jon and Dulcie go off by themselves—I mean we're not all joined at the kneecaps or anything, but mostly we all go places together or just hang out. We found this fabulous candy shop with homemade chocolate turtles to die for. Melt in your mouth, suffuse your whole being with warmth and joy. (I've always wanted to use suffuse in a sentence.)

One day when Dulcie and Jon took off on their own, Ted and Anthony came over and helped me paint my room—I decided on Rain Forest Green. Dulcie and Jon got here about five, and Carol ordered pizza and built the first fire of the season in the fireplace. AND she took both kids and left us alone. I think it was the best day of my life.

You can't really talk to guys like you can to a girl, but Ted and Anthony are okay. I think Hannah has a crush on them both. She's always hanging around.

I've learned something important: guys and girls can be just friends, meaning there doesn't have to be sex.

Love, Sara

P.S. Put my combat boots in back of the closet today. They don't fit with my look anymore. And they're too hard to dance in.

From: Dulciana Newton [DANcer@ezmail.com]
Date: Sun, 11 Oct 1998 13:10:15 EST
To: Sara Reichert [enigma22@ezmail.com]
Subject: babble

Hey Sara! That was really nice last night.
Sorry we didn't get back in time to help
with the paint. LOVE the color. It's gonna
be superchoice when you get done.

Jon went golfing with his dad—he hates golf
but his dad loves it, so. . . . I guess that's
the only thing his dad ever has time to do
with him. What a difference from my dad!
When I was about twelve, I had to beg to
stay home from the dealership—he was so
proud of me, it was embarrassing.

Guess nobody's ever satisfied. Wow! Am I
getting philosophical or what?

Tryin to get a head start on our next English
assignment. What do you think of an updated
Romeo and Juliet? I could tell it from the

parent peeps' point of view. That might
help me understand mine. :)

Omigod! It's snowing! It's too early for winter. Got to drag out my coat. Brrr. —Dulcie

----

From: Sara Reichert [enigma22@ezmail.com]
Date: Sun, 11 Oct 1998 15:20:34 EST
To: Dulciana Newton [DANcer@ezmail.com]
Subject: RE: babble

Hey, Dulcie,

Sorry it took so long. Carol decided to
take time off from her MCSE certification
studying, and we just got back from Holden
Arboretum. Keith insisted on walking one of
the trails by himself. And got lost, of
course. And Carol got nuts, of course. Why
does she want to go there?

Snow powdered sugar when it started, but by
the time we left, the flakes had turned fat
and lacy. 2 inches on the ground.

I like yer updated *R and J* idea, but it'd be
super-hard to write from that POV. You'd
always be writin the exact opposite of what
makes sense.

Anyway, got my furniture moved back this
morning. Pics of us from the RAINN Concert
party stuck up in the edge of my mirror.
Looking good! Hey, where did you guys go
y'day anyway? You looked so happy, I could
almost hear you purring.

Sara

From: Dulciana Newton [DANcer@ezmail.com]
Date: Sun, 11 Oct 1998 15:43:15 EST
To: Sara Reichert [enigma22@ezmail.com]
Subject: RE: RE: babble

Sara, SECRT SHIT, OK? We went to Jon's
house. Wonderful to be alone, just the two
of us, fire in fireplace, bottle of this
choice sweet pink wine. Sigh . . . Jon is so
gentle, and HE LOVES ME! You have to try it
sometime.

Dulcie

From: Sara Reichert [enigma22@ezmail.com]
Date: Sun, 11 Oct 1998 15:58:34 EST
To: Dulciana Newton [DANcer@ezmail.com]
Subject: RE: RE: RE: babble

NO THANK YOU! Pink isn't my color. And I
thought you hated sweet stuff.

From: jon draper [captainJ@ezmail.com]
Date: Thurs, 15 Oct 1998 18:15 EST
To: DANcer@ezmail.com,   enigma22@ezmail.
com,   lmbakert@abc.com,   xblader1@abc.com,
SCOOPer@ezmail.com,   GANDOLF@usalink.net,
tp108842@coolmail.net,   mrRogers@ezmail.
com,   unicorngold@ezmail.com,   HOTmustard@
abc.com,   rhett@ezmail.com,
Subject: PARTEE DOWN, party in jon's world,
party time, EXcellent!!!!

HO HO THERE, MY FUNKY KITS AND KITLETS.
It's official! Party time again at jon's
house. rents gave approval for the annual
bash at the farm, saturday after the St.
Ed's game, the 31st. Lookin for an excuse
to drop those books? hey, even brains and
pains gotta take a break sometime right?

yer at Jon's with a smallish load of peeps
just like yerself. It's a confluence around
a Bfire when the moon's full but MEN, yer
gonna wanna bring a flashlight cuz the home-
stead's awesomely big and top-shelf woman-
hunting ground. bring yer elephant ears cuz

Hot Mustard (Dancer's rockin band) is gonna play! If you sk8, bring yer shtuff cuz the rents sprung fer a ramp.

and yer gonna wanna be DRESSED and ready to be WHO? somebody else fer sur.

Note: Fer those of you buried in bks, it's the day when the dead walk, so come on up outta yer graves and dance. We gots SWING, if ya want.

Bring food! cuz otherswise—you don't eat. (hahaha) rents will go only so far, and jon's funds are pitiful. Bring yer baby sibs if yer up to it. since the baby cuzes are visiting, I had to invite 'em. We'll have a separate corral for the little pos- settes, or we'll tie 'em to trees.

HAHAHAHA.

RSVP to captainJ@ezmail.com or call at (216) 555-7654.

OK. luv you bubbys and bubbets.

From: Dulciana Newton [DANcer@ezmail.com]
Date: Thurs, 15 Oct 1998 19:11:49 EST
To: Sara Reichert [enigma22@ezmail.com]
Subject: jon's PARTEE

Sara

Isn't this awesome? Did you RSVP yet? Who
are you going to be? My first flash fer me is
Mae West—with a flowery hat and boa and huge
fake boobs and bushels of makeup 'n stuff.
What think?

D

From: Sara Reichert [enigma22@ezmail.com]
Date: Thurs, 15 Oct 1998 19:23:49 EST
To: Dulciana Newton [DANcer@ezmail.com]
Subject: RE: jon's PARTEE

Answers: yes. not yet. not sure. Mae would
be perfect for you. Maybe W. C. Fields for

94

me. Always wanted to have a big red nose and carry a cane. And didn't he hate kids and dogs?

But seriously, me—Prob'ly someone from a book—what do you think Holden Caulfield would wear—khakis, sht-kickrs, and an old t? Easy!

Sara

P.S. Where have you read this before?

<<*Good night, good night! Parting is such sweet sorrow / That I shall say good night till it be morrow.*>>

—William Shakespeare

My Journal, My Life

Cher Henri,

Big Halloween costume party at Jon's. Guess his folks have a "farm" in the country. Would you mind if I went as you? It would be so cool—no one would know me, and I could use Hannah's skateboard and shoot around the grounds on my knees with a paintbrush in my teeth. What do you think?

I'm excited, don't know exactly why. Guess it's that I've never gone to anything like this before. It sounds really great, with live music, and Dulcie's going to sing with that band. Of course the entire football team will be there, and I'll have zero in common with them—but Dulcie wants to go, so. . . . I'll keep you informed.

Bye for now, Sara

P.S. Hannah's favorite lipstick disappeared. You and I are the only ones who know what happened to it.

P.P.S.

"Law, Brer Tarrypin!" sez Brer Fox, sezee, "you ain't see no trouble yit."

—*Joel Chandler Harris*

My Journal, My Life

OCTOBER 17, 1998

Cher Henri,

You won't believe it! It's too awful. Hannah wants to go to the party, and Carol said I had to take her. Even if I don't go as you and borrow her skateboard!

Last week Hannah announced that she's letting her hair grow long, and today I noticed she's wearing my old green sweater. I thought I threw that out. What?! Does she think we'll be twins?

I'm trying to be adult about this, and it's not that I really hate kids, or anything. But HANNAH!!!!???? Maybe I will go as W. C. Fields and stay a hundred miles away from her.

At least Keith doesn't want to go. More later.

Love, Sara

From: Sara Reichert [enigma22@ezmail.com]
Date: Wed, 21 Oct 1998 20:16:54 EST
To: Dulciana Newton [DANcer@ezmail.com]
Subject: smiles

Dulcie

Okay, I'm excited about the party again.
I've been stayin cool and not sayin anything, and guess what? Hannah decided not
to go! Maybe becuz she knew I'd die if she
went? Nah—then she would have gone for
sure. Whatever—glory hallelujah! The gods
are smilin, yeah they are.

Me too: smilin big, lots of teeth, Sara.

Don't you love this?

<<Woman's mind
Oft' shifts her passions, like th'incon-
stant wind;
Sudden she rages, like the troubled main.
Now sinks the storm, and all is calm again.>>

—John Gay

99

From: Dulciana Newton [DANcer@ezmail.com]
Date: Wed, 21 Oct 1998 20:29:01 EST
To: Sara Reichert [enigma22@ezmail.com]
Subject: RE: smiles

All right! Your storm has sunk—that quote
is choice.

But what about this? Didn't hear from J all
weekend, plus he hasn't been in school for
3 days. Left a message on the machine but no
callback. I know he's busy 'n stuff, but
what's up with that? Afraid he's blowin me
off. Am I being possessive?

D

From: Sara Reichert [enigma22@ezmail.com]
Date: Wed, 21 Oct 1998 20:37:54 EST
To: Dulciana Newton [DANcer@ezmail.com]
Subject: RE: RE: smiles

No, you sound like a girlfriend.

S

From: Dulciana Newton [DANcer@ezmail.com]
Date: Wed, 21 Oct 1998 20:45:01 EST
To: Sara Reichert [enigma22@ezmail.com]
Subject: RE: RE: RE: smiles

So I'm just being stupid?

From: Sara Reichert [enigma22@ezmail.com]
Date: Wed, 21 Oct 1998 20:55:54 EST
To: Dulciana Newton [DANcer@ezmail.com]
Subject: RE: RE: RE: RE: smiles

No!

YOU are NOT stupid! Let's analyze this.
What happened the last time you saw him?
Did he ever tell you what the "thing" was
that happened, why he stopped seeing those
rich kids?

S

From: Dulciana Newton [DANcer@ezmail.com]
Date: Wed, 21 Oct 1998 21:03:01 EST
To: Sara Reichert [enigma22@ezmail.com]
Subject: RE: RE: RE: RE: RE: smiles

I'm afraid to ask about it. Everything was
so perfect with us, didn't want to tip the
Titanic.

D

From: Sara Reichert [enigma22@ezmail.com]
Date: Wed, 21 Oct 1998 21:11:54 EST
To: Dulciana Newton [DANcer@ezmail.com]
Subject: RE: RE: RE: RE: RE: RE: smiles

Okay, here it is—it's nothing. His family
probably just decided to jet off to New
York for "The Theatre" or to Paris to shop
or something, and they kidnapped him.

S

From: Dulciana Newton [DANcer@ezmail.com]
Date: Wed, 21 Oct 1998 21:19:01 EST
To: Sara Reichert [enigma22@ezmail.com]
Subject: RE: RE: RE: RE: RE: RE: RE: smiles

Should I call him again? Don't say, What do
you want to do? Okay, I'll call him.
Omigod—they're playing John Lennon's "I'm
Losing You" on the radio.

From: Sara Reichert [enigma22@ezmail.com]
Date: Wed, 21 Oct 1998 21:25:54 EST
To: Dulciana Newton [DANcer@ezmail.com]
Subject: RE: RE: RE: RE: RE: RE: RE: RE:
smiles

For God's sake change the station.

From: Dulciana Newton [DANcer@ezmail.com]
Date: Wed, 21 Oct 1998 23:10:15 EST
To: Sara Reichert [enigma22@ezmail.com]
Subject: excellent thing

Sara, you were right again. Heard from Jon
about an hour ago. Would have written right
away but had to talk to my dad first—more
about THAT in a minute.

Jon's parent-people are the pits. Anyway,
what happened: the whole family—all his
cousins, aunts, uncles, etc.—had to visit
the grandmother—his dad's mother. She's got
a cabin (I can just imagine) at the Eastern
Shore. (Nothing like the fishing cabin his
mother's mother—she died last year—had in
Vermillion. Guess that's totally primi-
tive.) Anyway, it was the dad's mother's
60th Bday and no one told Jon they were
going. He said he called here Sunday night
about 11:00, but my dad wouldn't let him
talk to me because it was "too late." I
could kill Dad for not telling me.

Anyway Jon wrote as soon as they got back. And he missed me. And he LOVES me.

So I'm flying again, watching the clouds down below.

Dulcie

From: Sara Reichert [enigma22@ezmail.com]
Date: Wed, 21 Oct 1998 23:26:54 EST
To: Dulciana Newton [DANcer@ezmail.com]
Subject: RE: excellent thing

That's horrible about J's parents, but what's up with your dad? What'd he say when you asked him?

Sara

From: Dulciana Newton [DANcer@ezmail.com]
Date: Wed, 21 Oct 1998 23:40:15 EST
To: Sara Reichert [enigma22@ezmail.com]
Subject: RE: RE: excellent thing

He is unbelievable, says 15 is too young to be seeing ANY guy, much less one who's almost 18. Says we have nothing in common with people like the Drapers. Don't want to hurt your feelings, Sara, but he sounded like you: "These people," he says, "don't care about anything but money and themselves." Guess Jon's dad was in court last year defending some big tycoon who fired a whole bunch of old employees.

Dulcie

From: Sara Reichert [enigma22@ezmail.com]
Date: Wed, 21 Oct 1998 23:51:54 EST
To: Dulciana Newton [DANcer@ezmail.com]
Subject: RE: RE: RE: excellent thing

That's absurd. Doesn't sound like your dad. Mine used to say, "Nothin ain't never what it seems." Guess he was right. About that anyway.

Anyway, it'll work out, your dad will change his mind. Hang in there.

Got to run, pick up Keith. Poor little guy's homesick and wants to come back early from his sleepover. I say freedom is a baited trap.

S

My Journal, My Life

Cher Henri,

Everything still going well, except for poor confused Hannah, who keeps "losing" stuff. She lost her house key yesterday, and Carol was not pleased. Asked if I was sure *I didn't know where it was.*

Of course I said I was sure. Even offered to give Hannah my key, if that would make Carol happy. I know I'm bad, but my ankh has not reappeared so . . . I told you I'd solve this my own way.

But "otherswise," as Jon would say, the world is in good order. He gave Dulcie a single white rose yesterday, and she brought it with her last night. She and I watched Sleepless in Seattle *for the twelfth time while Jon went bowling with Anthony and Ted. We used up about a box of Kleenex.*

Dulcie didn't want popcorn, said she felt "funny," like she might be getting a cold. Hope it's not that sore throat thing I had. I think what's really bothering her is Jon spending too much time lately without her.

107

Ted asked again the other day if I'd go to a swing club with him. I'm seriously considering it. Even if he'll probably step on my ankles.

He's a really nice guy, but kind of strange. He says that people don't question changes when they come along—technology and stuff—and that's why the world's so screwed up. Nobody thinks anymore. I just laugh at him, tell him he won't be happy until we all live in caves again.

Found out we made over two thousand dollars for RAINN at the party.

Speaking of Carol and everything going so well—I've been thinking of calling Mama. It's a big step, but my life isn't her fault; so many things in life are a mystery to her. I don't think she even knew what was going on with Daddy. She IS my mother and I don't hate her. I mean, I can't not talk to her for the rest of my life. This might be the perfect time. I'll let you know.

Later.

Love, Sara

P.S. Carol's studying is getting old—who knew you could get tired of pizza every night? She is totally out in some faraway galaxy. Hasn't asked me how I feel in weeks. And Keith wore two different shoes to school today. I'm the one who has to listen to Keith's long stories now—the ones that always start, "Hey, Sara, guess what." Sigh. . . . But he IS funny.

My Journal, My Life

Cher Henri,

Before I forget the details, I'm including this phone call between my birth father and me, because I think it's important. I don't know HOW yet, but I think it is. I was trying to call Mama this afternoon, but he answered.

> S.: *This is Sara.*
>
> D.: *Well, now, Sarie. How's my baby girl? You missing your daddy?*
>
> S.: *Uh huh. Is Mama there?*
>
> D.: *Nope, she's up to Archer's. Let me run out of beer.*
>
> S.: *Okay, I'll call back later.*
>
> D.: *You don't want to talk to your daddy? You been forgetting all about me?*
>
> S.: *No, of course not.*
>
> D.: *Got everything you want up there, do you? That woman taking good care of you?*
>
> S.: *Sure.*

D.: *When you coming to visit me?*

S.: *I don't think I'm allowed.*

D.: *Nobody here ain't going to tell them busybodies nothing. It's purely our business.*

S.: *I'll talk to Mama, see what she says.*

D.: *Now, I'll be looking forward to that. Ain't nobody can hug me like you, Sarie.*

S.: *I better go now.*

D.: *Your daddy loves you, honey.*

S.: *I know you do.*

My teeth chattered the whole time I talked to him, Henri, and I shook all over, even though it isn't really cold.

Sara

P.S. Later . . . couldn't sleep. Wrote this song:

"Barbed Wire"
(to the tune of "Dangling Conversation" by Paul Simon)

It's a cracking oil on canvas
of a mournful graveyard scene.
Let the system stand between us
and drop the guillotine.

And I grab and hold my anger,
as I hear your words again.

I'm a jaguar with a bleeding paw,
Wounded, tired, in pain.

I don't want to understand you.
There is no compromise.
That's barbed wire between our lives.

Now I've said good-bye to childhood.
It's too late, not one more chance.
You hold your arms out, want to hug,
but I leave without a glance.

I don't want to understand you.
There is no compromise.
That's barbed wire between our lives.

Henri, I HATE HIM!

Silent Auction

August 7 dawned hot and hazy, a perfect summer day. Fluffy white clouds floated across blue skies; the full, heavily blooming rosebushes, planted 135 years ago by the town founders, twined about obelisks and ancient trellises, filling the air of the park with sweet scent.

The children arrived first, shortly after noon. Some, yelling and laughing, ran for the Terrence Philip Rowen statue, the Gazebo, the Veterans' Memorial Wall, anything on which they could climb. On this, the second most exciting day of the season, next to July 4 and fireworks, summer still stretched infinitely, joyously ahead.

Older girls sat on wooden benches, chatting while they watched small brothers and sisters in shorts and sunsuits on the playground. Older boys hung on the high chain-link fence and stared out at the lake. Today the wind had whipped the waves into frothy ribbons that threw themselves one after the other at the foot of the cliff.

Younger boys pretended to open the fence gate and push one another through it, rolling on the lawn until they smashed on pretend rocks far below.

Soon, the men straggled in, full from their noon dinners, shaking hands as they gathered together by the old pin oak.

The women, most wearing jeans or shorts and cotton shirts, arrived in groups of two or three.

The people of Redwood were waiting, as their parents and grandparents had waited every August 7 in living memory, for one o'clock P.M. Children and parents together strolled to the massive restored Victorian home on the east side of the park.

The clock in the bell tower chimed, and blue-haired Mrs. Terrence Philip Rowen III threw open the heavy, carved wooden doors and walked out into the dappled sunlight of the wisteria-draped porch. The townspeople breathed.

As was the tradition, Mrs. Rowen gave a short speech in her reedy voice about Whitfield Carter Rowen, who settled in and founded Redwood, and held the first auction in 1860. "I am proud of my forward-thinking ancestors," she said, "and I am proud of you townsfolk for continuing our tradition. Because of you, we have never had a child at our home for longer than one year."

Applause. "This year, we have been home to only three children. I believe that here we are finally making some headway with this terrible problem which plagues our society. And now—the auction is open."

Applause.

Slowly the townspeople passed through the doors and climbed the center staircase, trailing their hands along the polished oak banister. Their footsteps followed the wide, picture-lined hallway to the three locked rooms at the back of the second floor.

A printed flyer decorated each door, side by side with a blank card for bidders' names.

The first flyer said,

ANTHONY
fifteen years old
parents killed in car accident
bed-wetter
violent temper
runs away

As people passed the room, they stared through the glass window strengthened with metal bars. All they

114

could see of Anthony was his back, and that he was a small boy with dull brown hair. When Tommy Morrissey said, "Hey, kid," Anthony gave Tommy the finger, but did not turn around.

At the next door, the flyer said,

RYAN
thirteen years old
extreme difficulty with bonding
father ran off three years ago
mother can't handle him, afraid of him

When the townspeople looked in this window, the boy Ryan faced them smiling. He wore a navy blue suit, white shirt, and tie. Tommy Morrissey elbowed John Baker. "He looks normal, don't he?"

But John noticed Ryan's eyes, the eyes that didn't have anything behind them, and stepped closer to his mother.

On the third door, the flyer said,

MELISSA
twelve years old
sexually abused by father
acts out with men and boys
has nightmares
lies

Melissa, a curly-headed, blue-eyed blonde, danced feverishly to music by Acid Nails, and waved to

115

everyone. She blew a kiss to John Baker, and he moved on quickly.

Soon, names appeared on all the cards. Tom Harmon bid six months of weekend labor for Ryan. "Good strong boy," he said. Clint Conner overbid Tom Harmon with a full year of weekends at the Rowen estate.

JoElle Campion bid a queen-size quilt for Anthony. "I think he's the one who needs the most help," she said. "You're right," Molly Walker said, and entered a bid of a king-size quilt *with* matching drapes.

Micki Newburgh, holding her smallest brother up to see through the window, looked at Melissa, and whispered, "It's a girl. A sister." Immediately, she wrote down her name and a bid of helping with next year's children for one year, crossed out the one year and made it two, and looked back at her parents who were smiling at Melissa through the window.

After all the bids had been made and everyone was back outside, a low hum filled the air as people talked and laughed nervously.

"I heard," said JoElle Campion, "that some towns quit holding the auction."

"Ridiculous!" said Mr. Baker. "What do they do with the kids then?"

JoElle shrugged. "Keep 'em till they're grown, I expect. The problems these kids have?" She shook her head. "Can you imagine keeping one for years?"

Then Mrs. Rowen stood at the door, her hand in the air, and the hum stopped abruptly.

"I won't keep you waiting," she said. "To those of you who have not made winning bids, remember that there is always next year.

"The winning bid for the boy named Anthony is from the Walker family."

The Walkers hugged one another, then Mr. Walker kissed his wife, walked up to shake hands with Mrs. Rowen, and disappeared inside the mansion.

Mrs. Rowen cleared her throat. "The winning bid for the boy Ryan is from the Clemons family."

Barb Clemons, a short dark woman, shouted, "Yes!" then clapped her hand over her mouth. She ran up the steps to Mrs. Rowen, waved to her girls, and went inside.

Micki Newburgh crossed her fingers and toes, wrapped her arms around herself, and held her breath.

"And the final winning bid for 1998," Mrs. Rowen said, "is from the Newburghs for the girl."

Micki's breath shot out in a rush. She gathered the boys into a tight circle and said a prayer as her parents, holding hands, stepped through the door. "Dear God," Micki said, "strengthen us to do what we have to do. Amen."

"Amen," the boys echoed.

Mr. Walker, Barb Clemons, and the Newburghs walked out of the house and into the sunlight, children in tow. The group was solemn-faced and still, except

Ryan who never stopped smiling, and Melissa who was dancing on her toes.

The Walker, Clemons, and Newburgh children ran to be with their parents and their new soon-to-be-adopted siblings.

Anthony was in a straitjacket. Micki knew that her new sister would not be any problem. She was so cute, dancing and snapping her fingers.

Mrs. Rowen smoothed her silk dress while she waited for attention to again return to her. "Winning families," she said in her thin voice, "we thank you for willingly assuming this tremendous responsibility.

"Remember, you have twenty-four hours, no more. Not everyone can be saved. If you cannot, with love and kindness, control your new child, you must return him or her. At noon tomorrow our town will again meet here, open the gate to the cliff, and share in the final disposition of that child. Good luck to you all."

Gradually the park returned to its usual natural isolation.

At the mansion, Mrs. Rowen stood, shoulders back, on the porch, staring out at the lake far below. For a moment, she rubbed her temples with her index fingers.

"Completely pointless," she said, turned, and entered the house. The carved wooden doors closed silently behind her.

CRITIQUE FROM CLARISSA BLAKE:

Sara,

Another strong A. I liked this a lot. You've picked up on Ms. Jackson's ability to use words that say one thing on the sunny surface of the story but, at the same time, give us a queasy feeling that there's something horribly wrong. You made me want to know more, to turn the pages without stopping. The omniscient narrator works well here, I think, and you've made us see a lot of characters without giving us too much of any one of them.

My only problem is with the climax. Exciting though it is, can you see how yours is different from/less powerful than Ms. Jackson's? I think you got scared. Someone has to die on the page, or at least, almost die, for "Silent Auction" to have that same power as "The Lottery." And in order for someone to die, you, the writer, must kill him. I know, I know, it's hard. But if you want to be a writer—no one ever said it would be easy.

Take my comments as you wish. If you choose to rewrite the ending, I'll give you twenty points of extra credit.

Would like to talk to you about this story. Come see me, okay? I promise I'll be there this time.

From: Dulciana Newton [DANcer@ezmail.com]
Date: Wed, 28 Oct 1998 19:10:15 EST
To: Sara Reichert [enigma22@ezmail.com]
Subject: What to do?

Sara, yer not gonna believe it! Finally, Jon told me. He walked in on his mom and dad talking. They'd been having their usual cocktails after his dad came home from work, and his mom says to his dad that she TOLD him not to let Jon go to that public school—she KNEW this would happen. She says, "The girl's father sells CARS, for heaven's sake. Can you imagine?"

His mother called me "a money-grubbing little Korean girl," and said they have to get Jon away from me. What is she talking about? I'm not Korean. I've been American since I was two, and what if I was Korean? Are Koreans ugly, or stupid, or something? And "money-grubbing"? What is that about? I don't need their money.

I feel like somebody socked me in the stomach, and Jon is fuming. He said it was like

121

when he brought Anthony home from school with him in 8th grade. His mom turned into the Ice Queen, told Anthony he wasn't welcome in her house. Jon is still totally embarrassed about it. And now this! That's why he couldn't tell me for so long what she said about me.

My life is turning to SHT.

Dulcie

From: Sara Reichert [enigma22@ezmail.com]
Date: Wed, 28 Oct 1998 19:20:34 EST
To: Dulciana Newton [DANcer@ezmail.com]
Subject: RE: What to do?

Oh, God, Dulcie. I can just hear that woman. Of course Jon is upset. Can he still keep seeing you? How can she hate you like that when she doesn't even know you?

Sara

From: Dulciana Newton [DANcer@ezmail.com]
Date: Wed, 28 Oct 1998 19:49:15 EST
To: Sara Reichert [enigma22@ezmail.com]
Subject: RE: RE: What to do?

Sara,

She didn't know Anthony either. I guess it
was enough for her that he wasn't white.
How can people be like that? It's so
totally ridiculous!

But Jon says she can't tell him who to see.
Tried to tell her he loves me, wants her to
meet me. I guess she wouldn't even listen,
went to bed with a migraine.

All I want is to be with Jon.

D

From: Sara Reichert [enigma22@ezmail.com]
Date: Wed, 28 Oct 1998 19:58:34 EST
To: Dulciana Newton [DANcer@ezmail.com]
Subject: RE: RE: RE: What to do?

D

What did Jon's dad say?

From: Dulciana Newton [DANcer@ezmail.com]
Date: Wed, 28 Oct 1998 20:10:15 EST
To: Sara Reichert [enigma22@ezmail.com]
Subject: RE: RE: RE: RE: What to do?

He just kept reading the newspaper. Jon
says if his dad had wanted to, he could've
stopped his mom cold, but he didn't say a
word. So it's the two of them against him.
Really, against us.

D

From: Sara Reichert [enigma22@ezmail.com]
Date: Wed, 28 Oct 1998 20:27:34 EST
To: Dulciana Newton [DANcer@ezmail.com]
Subject: RE: RE: RE: RE: RE: What to do?

Want to skip Jon's party?

S

From: Dulciana Newton [DANcer@ezmail.com]
Date: Wed, 28 Oct 1998 20:40:15 EST
To: Sara Reichert [enigma22@ezmail.com]
Subject: RE: RE: RE: RE: RE: RE: What to
do?

No Way! If we go, they'll HAVE to meet me.
I'll be their guest.

Anyway, I've got my "Mae" clothes together,
and I look GOOD! So we're goin! Three more
days till the meet, as they say on the cop
shows.

D

From: Sara Reichert [enigma22@ezmail.com]
Date: Wed, 28 Oct 1998 20:51:34 EST
To: Dulciana Newton [DANcer@ezmail.com]
Subject: RE: RE: RE: RE: RE: RE: RE: What
to do?

You go girl! You can do this! WE can do
this.

S

My Journal, My Life

SUNDAY, NOV. 1, 1998

Cher Henri,

About Jon's PARTEE: Unbelievable! I practiced skate-boarding on my knees for days. Carol and I went through every rack in five old-clothes stores to find a beret, baggy-sleeve shirt, and men's trousers. I borrowed a foot-long paint-brush from the art department to hold in my teeth and pasted on a mustache. I was a painting fool! And guess what.

Half the people didn't even wear a mask, much less a cos-tume. Me: Can you spell embarrassed?

There were two thousand little kids running around, and Jon's parents did the bob-for-apples thing for them, and one of his cousins held a little girl's head under water until she about choked to death, and then the girl started a water fight, and I got soaked trying to stop it.

Lots of the older kids (even Anthony making out with some girl I never saw before) ended up in the woods together, flashlights shining everywhere. And lots of people had bottles with them in brown paper bags, including Jon. I know because Ted talked me into going out there with him. When he took my hand, I left. Fast!

Some people didn't bring food, and one of the kids in Dulcie's band refused to play—said no one would appreciate his music—so nobody played. All they had was the sound system, and most of what they played was pop stuff. Can you spell mind-numbing?

Great roaring bonfire, but nobody spent much time around it except me. The skating ramp just stood there empty. Hannah would have loved it.

The absolute worst thing was this: Dulcie was stylin as Mae, but Jon did not introduce her to his parents.

I don't know how she kept from crying. At the end, her eyes didn't sparkle anymore like Mae West's. Instead they looked like a cornered rabbit's.

I hated for her to be in pain like that, and I couldn't do anything. God, I still can't.

What did I learn from this party? The most important person in your life had better be yourself.

Brr—that sounds cold. What I mean is: Here I was, following Dulcie up this mountain called life, climbing better than I ever have. And now, here's Dulcie—slipping, sliding down past me in slow motion, and I can't grab her.

Good night, Henri.

P.S. Stopped again to talk with Ms. Blake, per her request. Again there's a note on the door that she has a family emergency. Wonder what this time? Hear that both her boys are what they call "troubled kids." Sounds familiar. Is there a Mr. Blake? What's up with him? Does she have to do everything?

From: Dulciana Newton [DANcer@ezmail.com]
Date: Sun, 8 Nov 1998 21:10:15 EST
To: Sara Reichert [enigma22@ezmail.com]
Subject: Jon

Sara,

This is so totally ridiculous. I feel like I'm living out *Romeo and Juliet*.

Jon's mother just discovered that he's sneaking out of the house to see me. She must have lost all touch with reality, because she called my house.

Now MY mother is furious too. Rose and Margaret both here (I guess Mom called them) when I got home. Tried to explain about Jon and me but nobody listened, just attacked. I guess my sisters were perfect children, saints. Thank God they had to go back home at dinnertime to their perfect husbands and children.

Dinner sawdust. Couldn't even swallow.

Do M and D really think just because they said I can't see Jon again that I won't? I'd die if I thought that.

Now I'm sneakin out too—tonight after everybody's asleep.

Sara, I love him so much. What am I going to do?

From: Sara Reichert [enigma22@ezmail.com]
Date: Sun, 8 Nov 1998 21:16:54 EST
To: Dulciana Newton [DANcer@ezmail.com]
Subject: RE: Jon

Ugh! The whole scene sounds like vultures on fresh roadkill.

You and Jon love each other. In Shakespeare's time you would have already been married. But, hey! Remember that Romeo and Juliet are CHARACTERS. You and Jon are REAL, and your story isn't going to end up a tragedy. You're both smart—you'll find a way around it. Yer folks'll come around.

I'll hold a good thought fer ya both. Tell Jon I said drinking makes it worse.

Love, Sara

<<*Your children are not your children.*
They are the sons and daughters of Life's
longing for itself.>>

—Kahlil Gibran

From: Dulciana Newton [<u>DANcer@ezmail.com</u>]
Date: Sun, 8 Nov 1998 21:30:15 EST
To: Sara Reichert [<u>enigma22@ezmail.com</u>]
Subject: RE: RE: Jon

Sara, thank you. You are a *TRUE FRIEND*.

Dulcie

From: Dulciana Newton [DANcer@ezmail.com]
Date: Wed, 11 Nov 1998 21:10:15 EST
To: Sara Reichert [enigma22@ezmail.com]
Subject: More Jon

Sara,

Couldn't get out tonight to see Jon, so I
wrote a song.

   <<For Jon>>
   (to the tune of "White Rabbit" by
   Grace Slick)

   One touch is red satin
   and one's a wool shawl.
   And each gentle touch you give me
   is my favorite one of all.
   We two are one now
   in life's banquet hall.

   One day you are granite,
   the next a rolling sea,

132

And then a hot volcano,
bright sparks rain down on me.
Together forever
is our destiny.

In ages past, we two were one,
then split. They said we must.
You smell clean, a rain-touched garden,
and then celestial dust.
We lived one life,
back in love, back in trust.

Remember what the angels say:
Love is good.
Love is good.
Love is good.

From: Sara Reichert [enigma22@ezmail.com]
Date: Wed, 11 Nov 1998 21:46:54 EST
To: Dulciana Newton [DANcer@ezmail.com]
Subject: RE: More Jon

Dulcie,

You are the smartest, most talented person
I know!

In awe, Sara

How I Spent My Summer Vacation/Green Paint

Families like mine usually didn't get to take vacations at the beach.

And here we are, in a sunny two-bedroom cottage facing Lake Erie with a screened-in porch and a beach. I'd say a haunted cottage, but that sounds like I watch too many horror films.

But why did the Comptons, the people Mama works for, let us have it for the month? Why aren't they staying here like they usually do?

Daddy laughed at me when I asked, of course, but Daddy laughs at me a lot.

He is the best-looking, nicest, most wonderful daddy a girl ever could have. But he doesn't believe in anything you can't see.

Daddy doesn't even believe in God. "If there *is* a God," he says, "life is his big joke."

Maybe that's one reason why I can't get well. Daddy doesn't believe I'm sick!

Aunt Mamie says in a low voice, "Just being away from your mama has got to help."

Mama's having another of her attacks and will be at the hospital for a while. She says Daddy knows what's best for us. I don't remember her ever disagreeing with him.

I don't always agree with Daddy, but here I am at the cottage.

I can't expect Daddy to spend every minute with me. Since we've been here, I've written in this little notebook Mama gave me, every time I had a chance.

The cottage is all alone at the end of a road about twenty miles from Bono, Michigan. The driveway is lined with a split-rail fence covered with fluffy bushes of tiny red roses.

I don't like my room at all. I wanted to sleep out on the porch with the smell of honeysuckle and the buzzing of bees, and the pretty white wicker furniture, but Daddy said no, the night air was too cool and damp, and I would be too far away from him if I had a nightmare.

He says he wants me to rest and get well. He takes such good care of me. I feel so guilty sometimes, so ungrateful.

So here I am in a big airy room, with two side-by-side windows that open only enough for a cat to get through. They look out over the lawn and the beach.

I guess this was the Compton boys' room because they were "holy terrors," Mama said. Probably the Comptons didn't want the boys climbing out of the house in the middle of the night.

The paint on the walls is a sickly mint green, old and peeling, faded in some places. Someone—probably the Compton boys—had begun scraping off the paint, and the wallpaper under it, little by little, behind the dresser and the bed.

I don't know which I hate more—the paint or the wallpaper.

There comes Daddy. Must put this away.

$$\cdot \quad \cdot \quad \cdot$$

We have been here a week, and I'm more relaxed, at least most days. The nights are dark though. The blue feelings start about sundown.

Daddy doesn't know how dreadful it is for me. He knows there's no reason for me to suffer, and that satisfies him. It's stupid of me to make him miserable and worried.

I'm really getting to like the room, all except that horrid paint. There is a big dark spot on the wall (Daddy says it's just old water damage) that looks like a face with the cheeks pouched out and the eyes sunken in.

There's no rug in here, and the floor is scratched up like the bed. It looks like the Compton boys hated it.

On the wall by the dresser the paint is especially scary. In late afternoon, when the sun slants low, I see a weird, shapeless thing—almost like a girl with braids— hiding behind the paint.

I can hear Aunt Mamie in the kitchen now. She's so nice, coming by to fix me lunch every day. I can't let her find me writing—she thinks it's what makes me sick.

·   ·   ·

I'm getting cranky and nasty from not doing anything.

I cry at nothing, of course only when I'm by myself.

And I'm by myself a lot now. Daddy often stays overnight in Bono.

So I walk down to the beach or to the road once in a while, sit on the porch hidden by the honeysuckle, and lie down up here often.

I like my room now in spite of the paint. Perhaps *because* of it.

·   ·   ·

No one knows about the girl with the braids but me, and no one ever will.

I'm eating more now, and I'm less nervous. You wouldn't believe how much I look forward to every day.

I don't want to leave now until I have found out. There is a week more. That should be enough time.

.   .   .

Fog and rain for days now. Green paint even stranger now with no sunlight. And the dampness . . . while it was sunny, I didn't notice the smell. Now it's everywhere, gets into my clothes and hair like cigarette smoke.

I thought seriously of burning the cottage down to get rid of the smell.

Funny streak on the wall, low down near the woodwork. It runs around the room, goes behind every piece of furniture—a long, straight, even groove, as if it had been scraped over and over.

.   .   .

That girl with the braids gets out sometimes. I've seen her way off, far down the beach, creeping fast, like a crab at low tide.

.   .   .

Two more days to get the paint off the walls.

Girl with the braids begins to push against the paint. I run to help her.

I pull, she pushes. By morning we've scraped off yards of that paper and the paint with it. Stripped high as my head and half around the room.

Sun comes out. That horrid paint begins to laugh at me. I must finish.

•   •   •

This is last day, but it's enough. Daddy in Bono.

After breakfast, I lock the door, throw the key onto the porch roof. It slides off, hangs up in the honeysuckle.

I want to astonish Daddy.

All day I scrape. Arms and neck ache, burn.

Mad now, enough to do something desperate.

Won't look out the window. That girl's down there skulking from one bush to another.

My shoulder just fits in that long groove around the wall. I can't get lost.

I creep, shoulder in the groove, scraping the wall. Shoulder on fire now, red blotches—blood?—on my shirt. Ugly red splotches, too, in the long groove.

Why there's Daddy at the door!

No use, Daddy dear. You can't open it!

He pounds and yells.

"Daddy dear," I say, "the key is hung up in the honeysuckle."

Quiet.

Then, calm voice: "Open the door, my darling."

I say slowly, "The key is hung up in the honey-suckle."

I say it three more times. He has to go.

When he finds it, he comes in. I look at him over my shoulder. His face—odd.

"Oh, my God!" he says. "Oh, sweet Jesus!"

"I've scraped off most of it," I say, "so you can't put me back."

Daddy slides down the wall, and I creep around the room to him, then over him, and keep going.

CRITIQUE FROM CLARISSA BLAKE:

Sara. More good work. Another A!!!

Your images are wonderfully vivid, and your dialogue real and poignant. You've picked up Ms. Gilman's increasingly disjointed style that conveys the girl's (Ms. Gilman's woman) descent into madness. This, truly, is an <u>unreliable narrator</u>.

I think that there's more at work in your story than in Ms. Gilman's. It's clear to me that your girl and her father have more history together than you've told us. I think you may, therefore, want to/need to give us more clues as to the cause of the girl's depression. I think you know a lot about this girl that you haven't told us.

I'll be here after classes today. Please come see me. I need to know that you're okay.

My Journal, My Life

Thursday, November 19, 1998

Cher Henri,

A week till Thanksgiving. My favorite holiday it is NOT! This year, Carol is insisting that I go with her and the kids to the West Side Market. Every year she buys a ham and all the Thanksgiving dinner fixings and drops it off at one of the charities for some poor family.

I guess a lot of people get depressed this time of year, especially artists and other creative people. I never heard of Pedro Calderon de la Barca—he lived in the 1600s, and my quote book says he wrote this:

What is life? A frenzy. What is life? An illusion, a shadow, a fiction. And the greatest good is of slight worth, as all life is a dream, and dreams are dreams.

Wow! I mean, talk about depressed. This is profound stuff. Why don't they just do away with holidays altogether if no one is ever happy to celebrate them.

142

Same nightmare again last night—totally alone, no one to go to, black hole. Played some of my music; that always helps. Got up and wrote:

> *Sad weary soul stripped away*
> *By dangerous night.*
> *Oh, God! This is home.*

It was hours before I got back to sleep.

Better today, although Carol's giving me a hard time about spending so much time away from home. Said she misses me, likes to see my laughing face. How can she see me laughing or otherwise when she's holed up in her office all the time? I think it's that she wants me to do more around the house.

Can't she just be happy that I'm happy?

And Ms. Blake called Carol and said she's worried about me. Now, what is that about? I talked to her—this time, amazingly enough, she was in her office. I told her I'm writing about things in the past. Can't she see that? Why are adults always trying to get into your head? I'm fine, for God's sake.

Hey! Time for better news: Dulcie and I are on this great Messenger thing now. The Messenger tells you if your buddy is on the Internet, and then you don't have to send email. You hear this door creak open when your buddy gets on line. A little box pops up on our PC screens, and then Dulcie and I just type back and forth to one another in the box. When you get off, the Messenger slams the door—I mean you really hear it. I'll cut and paste the text into my word-processing program to save the messages I think might be important.

Got to run. You can't believe what a zoo this place is since Carol started studying for her certification stuff. A week of newspapers on the dining-room table. Dishes in the sink from breakfast. Coffeepot burned up today—she forgot to turn it off. Laundry hamper overflowing. So I know I could have helped out before, but I'm busy, too. Okay, okay. I'm on my way.

Your friend, Busy Bee Me,

Sara

November 28, 1998

Messenger

Sara: Dulcie—Thank God. Just saw that
you're on-line, right after the light
went on in your room. Where were you
today? Tonight? I was worried out of my
mind.

Dulcie: No time to explain. I need you.
Meet me in hlf hour? You're only one I
trust. You know where.

Sara: Slow down. I'll be there.

November 29, 1998

Messenger

Dulcie: Sara, the test is positive!

Sara: Are you sure?

Dulcie: I'm sure. Pink line in the right window, just like the box said.

Sara: How could you be so stupid?

Dulcie: Thnx. Just what I needed to hear.

Sara: Sorry, but I mean it. Don't you remember anything from Sex Ed? How many $$ is a condom? They're free from the school nurse, for God's sake.

Dulcie: We didn't mean to. It just happened.

Sara: Can you spell *ridiculous*?

Dulcie: Really! It just seemed right—two halves of a whole, together. Perfect. Never felt that way before—like being wrapped in a cocoon of silk.

Sara: Stop! Don't want to hear this.

Dulcie: You'll see. You don't know about sex yet, but one day, you'll be out with Ted and you'll find out.

Sara: WHOA! Where the hell did that come from? That is so wrong. You don't know everything about me.

Dulcie: I get it. You DID IT with Ted, didn't you?

Sara: NO!! Never! Forget it. I'll tell you some day. This is not about *me*. What are *you* gonna do? What's up with Jon?

Dulcie: Callin him right now. Hate to. He's real down, says his fumble lost the game last week, and I guess his dad thinks so too.

Sara: So what? Football's a damn game, not a world war.

Dulcie: I hear you, but it's life and death to them. Even if it weren't for that, I don't know how he can tell his parents about this. I can't tell mine. Could you tell Carol?

Sara: Be serious! She's already giving me a hard time about not talking to her enough, and I don't have anything to keep a secret about.

Dulcie: Exactly. And *she* knows *you're* not perfect. Not like my mom and dad and me. THEIR little girl would never do anything like this.

Sara: Sorry, got to pick up Hannah at her girlfriend's. Call me after, okay?

November 29, 1998—Later

Messenger

Sara: What'd he say?

Dulcie: He's wonderful. So smart. Says see a doctor first, then figure out what to do.

Sara: Good idea. Want me to go with you?

Dulcie: Thanks, but Jon'll take me over to the clinic tomorrow. Don't tell anybody, okay? Promise?

Sara: Promise.

November 30, 1998

Messenger

Dulcie: Life is a four-letter word!

Sara: What's wrong?

Dulcie: Just got back from the clinic.

Sara: What'd they say?

Dulcie: Confirmed kit test. I'm seven weeks.

Sara: Damn! What did Jon say?

Dulcie: He was so totally closed off when we went to the DRs. I haven't called him since he dropped me off.

Sara: Why not? You have to.

Dulcie: What if he

Sara: Don't stop typing like that. What if he what? It's his baby, he loves you, you'll get married. End of story.

Dulcie: We can't. His 'rents.

Sara: Yeah. With their money? They can take care of you till Jon finishes college.

Dulcie: But they won't. They hate me. He'll hate me. He

Sara: What? He had nothing to do with this? Got pregnant on yer own, did you? You make me so mad. You're creating a soap opera. Hey, this happens all the time. To lots of peeps.

Dulcie: Easy for you to say. You're not the one with the baby growing inside you, whose whole life is friggin chaos.

Sara: Sorry, Dulcie. Okay, I can't know how you feel. But I know Jon, and he'll stand by you. You hafta call him.

Dulcie: Right now?

Sara: Right now.

My Journal, My Life

NOVEMBER 30, 1998

Cher Henri,

You will cry when you hear this: Dulcie is pregnant. I know, I know. She needs me now, but I'm clueless how to help— probably because I'm furious with her. And hurt. Is it better to count on someone, or to be the someone being counted on?

Carol flunked her first certification test. Believe me, I know how she feels, but the world IS still in orbit. She's a zombie right now—eyes unfocused, mind gone (yesterday she let Keith make his own PBJ sandwich—you should have seen the kitchen after—and asked ME to get her beloved truck washed!). I have to remind her to eat; she studies all night, I guess.

I can't do everything, Carol.

P.S. Bandaged Keith's scraped knee yesterday, and he hugged me! And Hannah helped with the laundry today. Also got her to agree to load the dishwasher after dinner. I'm at a point where I kind of hate to keep on messing with her, taking her stuff, but she has to learn, right?

HONORS ENGLISH LIT/CREATIVE WRITING
ORIGINAL ONE-ACT PLAY
PREMISE: Jealousy destroys itself and the object of its
love.
December 4, 1998

Cuckoo Love
A One-Act Play
by
Sara Reichert

CHARACTERS:
Kate Wyler
Tiffany McCloud

SCENE: *Tiffany's bedroom, upstairs at the McCloud resi-*
dence. A blue canopy bed sits against one wall. Two windows
with white ruffled curtains overlook the park. One door leads
from the room to the hallway, one leads to the attached bath.
    Kate lies on the bed, leafing through a magazine. When
Tiffany enters the bedroom from the bathroom, she holds a

*small white strip of plastic in her hand. Kate drops the maga-
zine and jumps up.*

KATE: Pink stripe in the big window. I forget. What does
it mean?

TIFFANY: It's yes.

KATE: Why are you smiling?

TIFFANY: I can't help it. Please, Kate, don't be mad at me.

KATE: I AM mad. At you AND Steve. How could you be
so stupid? Whatever happened to our saying, "Zippers
up, girls"? What happened to "Condom first, boys"?
How could you let him—

TIFFANY: It wasn't like that.

KATE: Oh, I see. This is another virgin birth?

TIFFANY: That's not what I mean.

KATE: In Sex Ed class last year you said you could never
do THAT with anyone.

TIFFANY: No, I said that's how I'd know it was love—if I
ever WANTED to do that with someone.

KATE: Give me a break.

TIFFANY: I just love Steve so much, Kate. I can hardly
stand to spend a minute without . . . you don't believe
me, do you?

KATE: Go on. I'm listening. I'm waiting to find out what
love has to do with not using a condom.

TIFFANY: We have every other time.

KATE: Every OTHER . . . how many? . . . never mind,
don't tell me.

TIFFANY: We always used something except that one time, after I won the talent show, remember? I was so happy, and you had to go home, and I guess I just forgot.

KATE: Forgot!!! You mean you wanted sex with him so much you couldn't take one more minute—

TIFFANY: Stop it. You're trying to turn something beautiful into something ugly.

KATE: Sex isn't beautiful or ugly. Sex is sex—a physical act. Anyone can do it—animals, birds—

TIFFANY: Please, Kate. You're my best friend, and I love you.

KATE: Talk about manipulative. Let me see if I've got this right: You are making it with Steve. You get pregnant. And now you want me to figure out what you should do?

TIFFANY: Come on, Kate.

KATE: I'm serious. YOU have to decide what YOU want to do.

TIFFANY: I don't knowwwww. That's why I'm asking you. The only thing I know for sure is that I cannot tell my mom.

KATE: Okay, here's an idea. I'll stage a benefit to get you money for an abortion. Or I'll get Father Penkowski to take up a special collection at mass so you and Steve can go to Jamaica for nine months. Maybe you'd just like me to—

TIFFANY: Why are you being so hateful?

KATE: I liked us the way we were. Whatever happens now, you and I will never be the same.

TIFFANY: Oh God, I just thought about that girl in my eighth-grade class, who was pretty dim and had a few screws loose, and got pregnant. It might not have even been her fault, and we all felt sorry for her, but she had to leave school. And now here's me, with all the nuts, bolts, and screws any girl could want, and I have also totally messed up my life. AND Steve's. What if he hates me?

KATE: He loves you. And I'll help. You'll work it out somehow; I know you will.

TIFFANY: It's easy for you to be optimistic.

KATE: Okay, I'm going home to get two aspirin. Then I'm going to lie down and make my mind a blank. I don't know what I'll do after that.

TIFFANY: I'll call you later.

KATE: And say what?

TIFFANY: Kate, before you go, I need a hug from my best friend.

KATE: You just don't get it, do you? You destroyed us. And I don't have one spare hug to give.

CRITIQUE FROM CLARISSA BLAKE:

Sara,

A serious subject, with smart dialogue. But I'm not sure about your theme.

I don't think you can say that "jealousy" or "Kate" destroys what it loves, when you've made it clear that "Tiffany," at least in Kate's mind, has destroyed the girls' relationship.

Would this be better?: Stupidity destroys what it loves.

Do you see?

If this is based in reality, if you know someone like this who is in this trouble, please ask her to talk to me. Maybe I can help.

My Journal, My Life

Cher Henri,
Another phone call I think is important. This one's between Dulcie and me.

> *D.: I can't stand it. This is so hard.*
> *S.: What?*
> *D.: Jon wants me to have an abortion. I told him I couldn't, that we'd be killing our baby, that we had to take responsibility for what we did. But he doesn't get it, says it's the only way we can go on with our lives.*
> *S.: Damn!*
> *D.: He's right about one thing—if I had the baby, I'd have to tell my mom and dad. That'd kill them. I can hear my mom—"What would the neighbors say? Your grandparents?"—I can't do this all by myself, Sara. Will you help me?*
> *S.: You had to ask? Of course I will. The three of us will figure it out. You'll be all right.*

D.: *You think?*
S.: *Yeah, I do.*

Another shatter-my-world call, later this same day, from Dulcie.

D.: *Oh, Sara, how could Jon be so stupid?*
S.: *What happened?*
D.: *All this time, you've been telling me it would work out, and I believed you. I mean, I thought that, too, inside. I figured that the baby might even make it all right between our families. Now—*
S.: *For God's sake, Dulcie, what is it?*
D.: *Jon told his father about the baby, and his father threw him out of the house.*
S.: *What? So where is he now?*
D.: *At the Clariton at the I-90 exit. Jon told me once that for his whole life, the only person's approval he ever wanted was his father's. Now he's saying life is over for him.*
S.: *Oh, no!*
D.: *And it gets worse. Jon's father calls my father. My mom's hugging me and sobbing—wants to know what she did wrong. My dad just says, over and over, "We gave you everything."*
S.: *Oh, my God.*
D.: *I can't stand it. This is so much worse than I ever thought it could be.*

S.: I don't know what to do.

D.: Just listen. Nobody else does, even Jon. It's like I'm a little kid or something.

S.: Maybe Ms. Blake could help?

D.: NO! Jon doesn't want anyone to know. He'd hate it if he knew I told you. He says WE got ourselves in trouble; WE get ourselves out. Got to go now. I'm on my way to the motel.

S.: Call me the minute you get there?

D.: I'll try.

My Journal, My Life

Cher Henri,

I've gone too far this time. Carol is furious! When I got home from school, she was in my room, my stash of Hannah's stuff strewn on the bed.

She's holding a lipstick in one hand and Hannah's red patent-leather purse in the other. She has this look in her eyes like she doesn't know me.

Her voice would freeze boiling water. "Why?" she asks.

Of course I don't answer, just look out the window.

"I am so tired of this," she says in that same dead voice. "You don't tell me there's any problem. Worse, you say everything's fine, I should trust you. Then—"

She waves her hand like there's a mosquito by her ear. "Hannah's only twelve," she says. "How could you hurt her like this? Only the good Lord knows why she looks up to you."

She what? *I don't say anything. There's nothing to say.*

"You will apologize to Hannah."

Keith bangs the door open. "Mommy, Mommy, the buzzer's going off on the stove."

"Go turn it off. I'll be right there." Carol takes a deep breath. "You know there has to be punishment, Sara?"

I nod.

"Good. I'm too angry now to decide what. I'm afraid of what I'll say." She scoops up everything from the bed. "You're grounded, of course. You will go to school. You will come home. You will drive only to pick up the kids."

When she leaves the room, my knees unlock, and I collapse into my desk chair.

God, what is wrong with me? What did I think I was doing? I am completely hateful, an ogre, a monster. I know I should apologize to Hannah, but I can't. This is her fault.

No, it's not. It's mine. I stole her stuff. It's my fault if Carol sends me back. God, that black hole is opening in front of me. I deserve whatever I get.

What should I do, Henri?

What do I want to do?

I don't know. Yes, I do. I want to talk to Dulcie, my friend. But I can't.

I won't say "Good night," Henri. Because it isn't.

Sara

My Journal, My Life

December 7, 1998, 8:00 P.M.

Cher Henri,
Since it looks like I might not be here much longer, decided to
call Mama tonight. I won't do it again.

> *S.: Mama? It's me.*
> *M.: Sara? Honey, what's wrong?*
> *S.: Mama, can I come home?*
> *M.: What? No. I mean, they said you can't. I thought*
> *you were happy there.*
> *S.: I want to see you and Daddy again. Before—*
> *Could I just come for a little while? If you'll be there.*
> *M.: Better not. Daddy loves you, but they say it's*
> *wrong. That's why you were doing so bad at school*
> *here and all. I can't do nothing about it. I guess they*
> *know best.*
> *S.: Mama, how's Susie?*
> *M.: Fine, I guess. She probably don't remember noth-*

ing. People adopted her are real nice. That Carol going to adopt you?

S.: I don't think so. Wait. Are you saying you'd let her adopt me?

M.: It'd be better for you. You got a new life now. No reason you can't do good in school. You're smart, like Daddy.

S.: Mama, I love you.

M.: Better you don't call again, Sara. They know best.

Henri,

Why do people always *let you down?*

From: Dulciana Newton [DANcer@ezmail.com]
Date: Mon, 7 Dec 1998 22:12:03 EST
To: Sara Reichert [enigma22@ezmail.com]
Subject: Unbelievable

I didn't think anything more awful could happen, but now, Jon's father canceled his credit card, so the Clariton kicked him out. And he doesn't have any money, so he's staying at his grandma's old fishing shack in Vermillion. On my way out there. More soon. D

From: Sara Reichert [enigma22@ezmail.com]
Date: Mon, 7 Dec 1998 22:30:00 EST
To: Dulciana Newton [DANcer@ezmail.com]
Subject: RE: Unbelievable

Should I meet you? Give me directions, say the word, I'll be there. S

My Journal, My Life

Cher Henri,
  I hope I've got every word right in this phone call from Dulcie.

  D.: *Sara—*
  S.: *Dulcie, I've been so worried. Where are you?*
  D.: *At the fishing cabin with Jon. And I . . .*
  S.: *What?*
  D.: *I wanted to write you, it would have been easier, but . . .*
  S.: *What would have been?*
  D.: *Please, just listen. I'm trying. Jon is so clear about this, and I love him so much. We have to be together.*
  S.: *Of course you do. What are you talking about?*
  D.: *Please, Sara. We're all right. We've made a decision, about what to do. And it's so much better now.*

165

S.: *For God's sake, Dulcie, what? What are you going to do?*

D.: *This is OUR problem, Jon's and mine, and we're going to take care of it.*

S.: *What happened to our being friends?*

D.: *You're making this so hard, Sara. There's nothing any of us can do about it.*

S.: *Dulcie, I—*

D.: *I have to go now.*

S.: *Will I see you at school in the morning?*

D.: *I don't know.*

S.: *You're scaring me, Dulcie.*

D.: *I'm fine. Bye, Sara.*

My Journal, My Life

Cher Henri,

Need to sleep, but HAD to write this. And you're the only one I trust to read it.

Scraps of Me

by

Sara Reichert

Why do I hate you? At last, a light shines:
you used my love, my innocence. "Taboo,"
they said. "A sin that can't be named." But you,
you named that sin. Each night you showed me death
and crushed my dreams with ogre-hands and
     bourbon breath.
Each day, your too-wide smile and ice-blue eyes
     replay,
B movies in my mind, ruin life today
for me, not you. No friends, no trust, no love

will ever come to me. Daddy, I'd shove
you from my waking thoughts. I can't forgive,
but you must stay, or who am I? I want to live.
What scraps of me are left behind?

Adieu, Henri

P.S.

> *Children begin by loving their parents; after a time*
> *they judge them; rarely, if ever, do they forgive them.*

—Oscar Wilde

P.P.S. Ripped up the only photo I had of him. Felt good.
Stared at the ones of Mama and Susie for a while, then put
them back under my shirts in the drawer.

No longer angry with Dulcie.
Just wish I could help.

My Journal, My Life

WEDNESDAY, DECEMBER 9, 1998

Cher Henri,

I'm so confused. In addition to everything else, I have PMS. I'm bloated, my head aches, and I got home from school hours late. Carol was steaming like a teakettle, and I don't even blame her. This time, she will send me back. I know it.

This was the longest day of my life, but where to start telling you about it?

Dulcie was in school today (skipped yesterday, called in sick), or at least her body was. She looked totally calm, as if she were lying in the sun at the quarry without a care in the world. She avoided me all day, and I was in a panic. But I skipped last period, ran home to get the car, and went back for her. I just INSISTED on going with her to see Jon, and she couldn't say no.

On our way to Vermillion, some guy plows through a stop sign on Route 6. I swerve to miss him, Dulcie screams, and the car skids into a light pole. Nobody's hurt, but the front fender is history. It's lucky the car's driveable. I mean, you could say it isn't my fault, but remember, I'm grounded.

I never even called to tell Carol. How could I? I forgot I was supposed to be picking up Hannah, who therefore had to walk home in the cold and almost-dark and . . . I am evil sometimes, Henri. I hate myself, so I know Carol does.

Anyway, when we get to Jon's grandma's cabin, I can't believe how rude it is—no heat, no stove, no paint. Jon's sleeping bag's in a corner next to a batch of stacked-up fishing rods. He's not happy to see me, but he offers me a beer, which I refuse. There are three empty bottles by the door.

I'm all prepared to hate Jon, but he looks like a zombie— dark circles, keeps one arm around Dulcie the whole time, just hangs on like he'll fall if he lets go of her. He's not even wearing his varsity sweater. When he spills his beer at one point, and just runs one finger through the puddle, I know he's really screwed up. The two of them just sit there, like they're dead.

I look from one to the other. "So what are you going to do?"

And Jon says, "It will be better for everyone if we're gone."

I freeze. "Gone where?" I look at Dulcie.

She takes my hand. "I told you, Sara. We've made our decision. Jon's right. No one will have to know about the baby if we're dead."

I freak.

"Dead?!" I yell, and shove Dulcie away. "What are you talking about? What about me? I know about it. Besides I thought you didn't want to kill the baby. Now you're going to kill yourself AND the baby." I am so loud, I finally hear myself. Screaming doesn't help anything.

I gulp some thin air. I shake all over, but I stop yelling.

Then Jon and I start talking at once, but I overtalk him, tell him how stupid that would be, how selfish. "You're angry now, and hurt," I say, "but you won't feel like that tomorrow."

"You don't know my dad," Jon says. "He never forgives anyone."

I touch his arm. "But you're not anyone; you're his son."

I notice that Jon's eyes are red. "Listen, Sara," he says, "my dad is worth a lot of money. I don't even know how much. But twenty years ago, his partner cheated him out of two thousand dollars. Two thousand measly dollars, and my dad hasn't talked to the guy since. To my dad, that guy is the enemy. Now I've crossed my dad—I am, too."

Dulcie takes his hand.

I sit back. "But your mom, Dulcie."

Dulcie shakes her head. "She's already planning for me to go to some place in Arizona called Friendly Haven for Unwed Mothers. She's already contacted adoption agencies. I'll never see Jon again."

"That doesn't make sense," I say. "NEVER? What's the longest it could possibly be—seven months?"

Dulcie frowns. "Please don't argue about words, Sara. You know what I mean. In seven months, the world will have changed."

I take a couple of deep breaths, think for a moment.

"Nothing's bad enough to kill yourself over," I say slowly. "I used to think about it a lot. When I was little, and Daddy was coming to my room every night, and I couldn't believe it would end. I even tried it once after some people I thought were going to adopt me sent me back to Elmwood instead."

I feel my hands tighten into fists.

Jon puts his arm around my shoulder, and Dulcie hugs me. "Oh, Sara. All that time we worked on the RAINN benefit, and I never knew."

"Look," I say, "I was glad, after, that they stopped me. Things got better for me. They will for you, too. I promise."

Jon's arm tightens around me.

"You can't make that promise," he says. "Life changes too fast. Look, my dad just canceled my gas credit card, and my car's sitting out there with less than a quarter tank. How could I support a family? All I see ahead for us is a filthy, roach-filled apartment, working some dead-end jobs like sweeping floors or washing dishes, us hating each other and the baby. I can't live like that."

"We're going, Sara," Dulcie said.

I thought about what I'd learned at the hospital after my suicide attempt. I wanted to make a list of ten alternatives, but couldn't come up with even one.

Anywhere you look, Henri, they're trapped. His parents, school, her parents, the baby. Everything's out of control.

"But there has to be something," I say. And I think, What? What could you possibly do to help? Talk to Carol? I don't think so! Not now! Recommend a priest? What priest? Ms. Blake? What could she do?

"You cannot do this," I say slowly. "I love you guys. You can't leave me here. I can't be alone again."

"And we love you," Dulcie says. "But you're not alone. You have other friends, and Carol—"

I shake my head. "I didn't want to bother you with my shit." I take a deep breath. "She's sending me back to Elmwood."

"She'd never—"

"Oh, yes. Yes, she would." I think about the car and Hannah and being grounded, and I stare at a spider climbing the window.

Dulcie grabs my hand. "Oh, God, Sara, I'm so sorry."

She looks at Jon and he nods.

We were alone, the three of us, no world beyond us. Out there was dark, cold. Together we were in light and warmth, at peace. This was love, Henri. Finally, I knew it, I felt it.

I shivered then. I shiver now when I think about it. The good kind of shiver like when something you read touches you deep inside.

It might sound stupid, Henri, but I am free now.

I can't live without them. I don't have anyone else, and I don't have any answers.

So we'll go together. Tomorrow. Jon's parents will be gone, and he still has a key to the house and his mother's car. Jon says that car fumes are the easiest way to do it—you just fall asleep and that's it. The next twenty-four hours are going to be hell. But we're going to end this mess. Together.

It's time to say good-bye now.

HONORS ENGLISH LIT/CREATIVE WRITING
OMNISCIENT NARRATOR
IN THE STYLE OF SHIRLEY JACKSON,
INSPIRED BY HER SHORT STORY "The Lottery"
NEW ENDING TO "Silent Auction"
Second-term Assignment: December 9, 1998
Original story date: October 23, 1998

(Ms. Blake: Omit everything after "Gradually the park
returned to its usual natural isolation.")

The next day, Mrs. Newburgh stood off to one side of
the crowd, staring through the chain-link fence at the
lake far below. Melissa, the child, chattered constantly
and danced around her like a cabbage moth.

Don Roberts called out, "Old man couldn't make it,
eh, Mrs. Newburgh? What a wuss." His wife punched
him in the arm, and the crowd laughed.

Mrs. Rowen opened her front door and waited until
the crowd hushed. "All right," she said, "are you ready?"

Mrs. Newburgh opened the gate. She tugged Melissa through it, and to the top of the cliff.

In her reedy voice, Mrs. Rowen said, "All right now. Let's do our duty quickly so that we can all return to our homes for lunch."

Someone, maybe Don Roberts, tugged Melissa's arms from around Mrs. Newburgh. Dorothy Hanfield pulled Mrs. Newburgh back to the fence.

The crowd, as if all the individuals in it had melded together into one force, surged forward.

Melissa's scream lasted only a moment.

"Thank you everyone," said Mrs. Rowen. She turned and entered her house, the carved wooden doors closing silently behind her.

The End

Thanks, Ms. Blake. For everything.

FINAL NOTES.DOC

Carol,

I'm sorry. Your home is the first safe place I ever lived, and I screwed everything up. Thanks for trying.

I know you won't understand, but you and the kids will be better off.

I love you, Carol. You're the first parent I ever said that to.

Dear Hannah,

Sorry I took your stuff. You can keep my ankh.

Give Keith my camera when he's old enough.

Ignore the kids who laugh at you. You'll find out who your real friends are. Remember, nothing's forever.

Dear Keith,

Don't be sad. Someday, when you're not mad at me anymore, ask your mom for a picture of me.

You're the best brother I ever had.

My Journal, My Life

DECEMBER 10, 1998

Cher Henri,

Can't think. Head pounding. Printed notes and "Auction" revisions. Signed notes.

Yesterday, I wanted to die with Dulcie and Jon. My friends, my only friends.

Have to do this.

I'm such a coward. I want to be with them. I don't want to die. How can I do this? What should I do? I hear you, Henri. What do I want to do?

I want to go back to the first day of school. Start over. No, the day before, keep Jon from meeting Dulcie.

I want to kill their parents. It's all so stupid. If only Dulcie weren't pregnant.

· · ·

This headache. Can't think. Eyes dry as fish scales. Stomach hurts.

· · ·

Later.

Threw up. Took nap. Nightmare again.

Carol still furious with me. Said she can see there's something wrong. Screamed at me (she never screams), "Why won't you talk to me?" Made me sit at the table even if I didn't eat. Or speak.

I know she cares. Why can't she understand?

I hear you, Henri: How can she? You don't tell her anything. Instead of writing some stupid note, why don't you tell her.

You're right. But how can I? If I told her what I think, how I feel, what would she do?

Could she be angrier than she already is?

I'll never know, will I? I'll never know anything after tonight.

After tonight, I won't exist.

• • •

GOD, I CAN'T DO THIS.

I can't kill myself.

I don't want to die.

I don't want Dulcie and Jon to die.

Death isn't the answer to anything, is it, Henri? Death is just death.

I have to stop them. I will stop them.

Maybe I should talk to Carol. Even though she hates me, maybe she would

Omigod. The time.

My Journal, My Life

Just got home. Sat at the hospital for hours. Doctors in and out. Police back and forth.

Everybody talking, talking, talking.

Police there when I got back. Carol found my suicide notes.

I HATE THEM. I'LL NEVER FORGIVE THEM.

So tired.

> *Regions of sorrow, doleful shades, where peace*
> *And rest can never dwell, hope never comes*
> *That comes to all.*

—John Milton

THE HOME DAILY

TWO WESTVIEW HIGH TEENS KILLED IN COLLISION WITH TRAIN

By Mark Roscough

WEST—Two Westview High School teens, one of whom was the football-team quarterback, were killed yesterday when a freight train slammed into them as the driver tried to beat it at a Columbia Avenue railroad crossing.

"This young man was playing Russian roulette with the train and he lost," said Michael Thomas, a gas-station attendant who witnessed the 7:05 P.M. crash from the nearby Marathon station where he was on duty. "What stupidity."

Police were called to the scene at apparently the same time that detectives were taking a stolen-car report from one of the parents.

Jon Draper, 17, and Dulcie Newton, 15, became the second and third Westview students to die during this school year. Draper's football teammate, Tim Willis, was killed in a car crash in September.

Draper was pronounced dead at 7:49 P.M. and Newton at 8:13, after both were taken by ambulance to Lake West Hospital in Lakeshore.

An autopsy was scheduled for today by Coroner Dramee Singh.

My Journal, My Life

Cher Henri,

Now that I can see through the broken glass in my eyes, let me fill you in on last night.

It was hard to tell in all the confusion when I got to the Drapers, but I guess Jon's folks came back early because his mother had a headache. They must have opened the garage door with the remote just as Dulcie and Jon were getting into his mother's car.

When I got there, Mr. Draper yells at me, wants to know what I know about their stealing the car. I try to tell him they weren't, but he's screaming again, ignores me, calls the police.

I run back home. At that time, I thought everything was okay—Dulcie and Jon had been stopped from suicide without my having to say a word.

When I rush into the house, Carol is on the phone, her eyes blank, pieces of paper crunched in her hand. Then she focuses, sees me. Her hand goes to her mouth, the papers float to the floor.

"Oh, my God," she says, staring at me.

I don't know, nobody does, if Jon and Dulcie wanted to be hit by that train.

The doctor kept me in the psycho ward at the hospital until this morning, until they were sure I wasn't going to kill myself.

When I get home, Carol hugs me until I think she's going to strangle me, and two seconds later, there she is—right in my face. She says not to bother ever thinking about committing suicide again, to just let her know and she'll kill me.

I say, "Your life would be easier, wouldn't it? If I were dead."

She says, "WHAT?"

And, in a second, we're both out of control. I remember yelling that I would NEVER be her daughter. And her yelling back, "Why would I WANT you to be?"

All this ugly stuff pours out of my mouth like I have nothing to do with it.

At some point, I realize it's only me yelling. Carol is saying things like, "It's all right. Get it all out. It'll be okay."

When I stop, I'm shaking. I wonder if Elmwood will let me out for the funerals. Carol wanted to get inside my head, I think, and now I've let her.

The rest of our conversation is burned into my brain.

Carol says, "I asked you to be honest didn't I? And you were."

From the corner of my eye, I see her take a deep breath.

"Promise me something?" I notice that her lips are turned up slightly at the corners.

I look at her. "What?"

"I'm really good at handling daily battles," she says, "but next time? Don't give it all to me in World War Three, okay?"

I nod.

"One question," she says, "before I go check on the kids who are probably wondering if we're killing each other. What would EVER make you think I'd send you back to Elmwood?"

I poke at a hole in my jeans. "Everybody else did. This time I know what I did wrong. Why wouldn't you?"

Her hand moves toward me, then stops. "Because I love you," she says.

My eyes sting. Keep this up, I think, and you'll have me crying like a baby. I press my lips together so my chin will stop quivering, and sit on an arm of the sofa.

She doesn't do anything stupid like hug me, just smoothes my hair on her way past. "Get some rest, dear heart," she says.

I couldn't hold back the tears anymore.

My Journal, My Life

December 11, 1998, Late

Cher Henri,

This afternoon Children's Services came around. They threatened to take me away, to have me declared incorrigible. But Carol begged, and I promised, and they're going to let me stay, for now.

Tonight at a family meeting, I apologized for all the trouble I'd caused.

Hannah told me I better never do it again.

Carol said she realized she couldn't change the big stuff in my life—like my past—so she'd been foolishly concentrating on the little stuff. No more micromanaging, she said, if I agreed to talk to her about my feelings. I agreed.

Keith—who ripped the eyes out of Harry, his favorite stuffed bear, that night—wants to have a funeral for him.

Still the same questions, Henri:

Did Dulcie and Jon mean to do it? I cannot believe they did.

Why didn't I get to the house earlier?

Good night, my friend.

Sara

P.S. God, I miss Dulcie.

P.P.S. Carol says that everything happens for a reason, and that no one can be responsible for anyone's life but her own. She believes it was an accident.

My Journal, My Life

Cher Henri,

Mortuary today.

The sickening sweet flower smell hits me in the lobby. My hands sweat in the too-hot room. I'll never look at a basket of white roses without thinking of this day.

At Dulcie's casket, the world stops—no sound, edges blurred and dark. I'm wrapped in an eggshell, a separate space holding only Dulcie and me. I cling to the kneeler, hear Carol from far away—"deep breaths."

Make myself look at the face. It's a cartoon—bloated, thick beige makeup. Dulcie never wore red lipstick in her life!

Dulcie's mother says something I don't hear.

I say what Carol told me people say at funeral homes, How sorry I am, how I'll never forget them.

I make myself go with Carol to Jon's casket. I've never seen his body still like that. And in a suit!

This isn't Romeo and Juliet. *This is real death.*

I feel a scream build in my head.

189

I concentrate, swallow, so I won't throw up.

When I got home, the first thing I wanted to do was tell Dulcie all about it.

Sara

P.S. Carol fixed macaroni and cheese from scratch—my favorite—for dinner.

My Journal, My Life

Cher Henri,

Funerals today. Dulcie and Jon gone. I'm still here.

Hannah saw the Drapers and the Newtons TALKING TOGETHER yesterday at the drugstore. I'm sick. And ANGRY!

Sara

> So with love—
> Sighs from the deep sea of affection;
> Laughter from the colorful field of the spirit;
> Tears from the endless heaven of memories.
>
> —Kahlil Gibran

My Journal, My Life

December 16, 1998, 11:00 p.m.

Cher Henri,

The coroner ruled Jon's and Dulcie's deaths accidental.

Why can't everybody be as wonderful all the time as they were tonight at the memorial service? Beautiful—hundreds of candles in the darkness. Fills me with hope.

I kept thinking how Dulcie would have loved it.

Sara

CRITIQUE FROM CLARISSA BLAKE:

January 8, 1999

Sara,

I have one word for your new ending to <u>Silent Auction</u>: Excellent.

The additional twenty points are yours.

You are an amazing, courageous girl.

My Journal, My Life

JANUARY 23, 1999

Cher Henri,

Sorry, but writing is like slogging through snowdrifts. I listen to my music and think of Dulcie.

Wandered downstairs last night about ten o'clock. Carol turned off the TV, made cocoa. We talked about life and love and God and pain until after midnight.

Sara

My Journal, My Life

MONDAY, FEBRUARY 8, 1999

Cher Henri,
  Finally said good-bye.

> *Happiness is a butterfly, which, when pursued, is*
> *always just beyond your grasp, but which, if you will*
> *sit down quietly, may alight upon you.*

—Nathaniel Hawthorne

  I'm sitting quietly.

Sara

My Journal, My Life

Cher Henri,

Once in a while I have a good day, well not a whole good day but . . .

> *for henri*
> *i'm struggling to understand why I write to you—*
> *therapy or ego, open wound or fright—*
> *could it be all the things you're teaching me*
> *like to laugh at my strange life, breathe naturally?*
> *you saved me, friend, from myself*
> *yeah*

Sara

P.S. Let Hannah wear my ankh yesterday.

My Journal, My Life

Cher Henri,

I might finally be waking from my zombie state. Stared at the photos in my album, and thought about Dulcie and Jon all day. Scraped myself raw inside.

Was it only two months ago I was totally alone, at the edge of a cliff? Today, I'm glad I'm alive. I want to shake Dulcie and Jon until their brains rattle in their heads.

Oh, and Carol asked if it was all right with me *if she filled out adoption papers when Children's Services gives the okay. Is it all right with ME? What do YOU think?*

Therapy today. It's kind of like having a garage sale—you sort through everything, keep the good stuff, and get rid of the junk. Of course, in therapy, you don't try to sell your junk to somebody else, but you get the point.

That post-traumatic-stress thing is probably what made me think dying would make the bad times go away, would mean they never happened.

But they did.

I can't throw Mama and Daddy away, but I can get rid of all that junk they gave me.

Good night, Henri.
Love, Sara

P.S. Just ran across that Martha Collins poem, "The Story We Know." Remember the first line?

The way to begin is always the same. Hello,

My Journal, My Life

Cher Henri,

    Met Ted and Anthony at the Common Ground last night.

    It's weird—everything the same, but not. We're trying not to talk about THEM. A girl in black reads some not-very-good poems by the light of a few flickering candles. We sit in the dark, breathing in the smoky air, sipping the hot bitter coffee.

    Ted breaks the ice when he spills his, and tells us he's done it on purpose, in memory of Jon. We laugh so hard that I get the hiccups. When was the last time that happened?

    Other people came over to our booth—girls and guys— and Ted kept me from getting wobbly.

    Here's what I think: As long as you're alive, I guess you've got a shot at life getting better.

    All right, all right. Not I guess. I KNOW.

Love, Sara